Shari Penny began a career that has spanned over 60 years as an entertainer, traveling all over the U.S. and Europe. She has hosted two television shows and found that her horizon had extended beyond what she could ever imagine. Her grandmother's stories proved to be a good source for the foundation of this novel.

Shari has two talented sisters, a brother who has passed, three amazing children, a large extended family and is a proud grandmother and great-grandmother. She is now working on a second novel, always focusing on love of family and positive moral lessons.

THE ENCHANTED CAROUSEL

Shari Penny

THE ENCHANTED CAROUSEL

Vanguard Press

VANGUARD PAPERBACK

A CIP catalogue record for this title is
available from the British Library.

ISBN 978 1 784655 67 9

Vanguard Press is an imprint of
Pegasus Elliot MacKenzie Publishers Ltd.
www.pegasuspublishers.com

First Published in 2019

Vanguard Press
Sheraton House Castle Park
Cambridge England

Printed & Bound in Great Britain

Dedication

To my wonderful family... those who have already passed and those who are still here. My sweet grandmother, Sydney, planted the seed for this story when I was just a little girl. She was a Southern lady who believed that grace and class were important parts in developing a young girl's character.

To my sisters and brother, my children, grandchildren, great-grandchildren and my extended family who have always thought I could do anything! Thank you for your belief and support, helping me keep on target with the times. You have made me extremely proud.

To the love of my life, Hank, who was married to me for over a quarter of a century and was my biggest cheerleader. Thank you for always being there for me then, and now, from the other side.

I love you all very much.

Prologue
Atlanta, GA – 1950

A somber rainfall followed the black hearse through the cemetery, as if the sleek and sorrowful vehicle dreaded the end of the journey. A procession of cars trailed behind like an angry river, filled with tears of sadness and grief. Many of the young adult mourners, some with children and others alone, looked stunned, not knowing how to accept the reality. The sound of umbrellas snapping out and car doors being opened and closed broke the awkward silence.

Eleven-year-old Crystal Baxter stood beside two graves under a green waterproof canopy as she twisted her short blonde curls nervously through her fingers. She searched the crowd and then lowered her head. Her words were barely audible. "Mother. Dad." She clutched two yellow roses. The thorns cut into her hands, but she hadn't noticed.

Two granite headstones positioned side-by-side read:

Margaret Lynne Baxter, 1915-1950, and Carter Taylor Baxter, 1913-1950.

She walked toward the graves, opened her hand

and allowed the flowers to drop onto the caskets. Her body shook as they landed.

An older woman who had been standing nearby gently took her hand and led her away.

*****

Crystal, still dressed in black, sat alone on the porch of a beautiful antebellum home. The heavy rain fell on the house's tin roof. Huge, dark clouds in the distance promised to head her way, and the wind howled through the trees, making an already bad day worse. No sounds of laughter or music could be heard, no sunshine appeared, just terrible dark skies and the rumble of distant thunder. How could things get any worse? She stared at the trees, listening to the frogs and birds. Didn't they know this was a sad day? Why were they singing and croaking?

She clutched a crystal horse pendant that hung from a golden chain around her neck. This special gift, made from a unique piece of crystal and faceted in precise detail was one of her most prized possessions, and she never took it off. She released her hold on it, took a deep breath, and began to relax a little.

Bertha, the same older woman from the cemetery, stepped onto the porch. Her grandmotherly face smiled faintly. She obviously cared for the young girl but didn't know how to make things better. She moved laboriously with each step until she reached the young girl and stood beside her.

"Honey, I made some fresh-squeezed lemonade and your very favorite oatmeal and raisin cookies."

The girl shook her head. "I don't ever want to eat again. I just want to die."

"Your mom and dad are happy because they are together. They still love you very much and always will. I promise, I'll tell you a story later. I know you may think you're too old for such things, but you always loved this one."

The girl finally smiled. "A 'once upon a time' story? The one you used to tell me, about the white horse?"

The old woman nodded and kissed her on the top of the head. "I love you so much. You'll see. We'll have fun living here together, and you'll make lots of new friends." She stood still for a moment and then turned away. With slumped shoulders, she pushed open the screen door, stepped inside, and allowed the door to slap shut behind her. She turned to look at the child who was everything to her. The young girl caught her eye, but immediately turned away and grasped the crystal horse once more.

At that moment, a large raven landed on the porch railing. He spread his black plumage and squawked loudly at Crystal. The raven, long-

11

considered a bird of ill omen and of interest to creators of myths and legends, didn't appear threatening as he walked toward her.

Unafraid, the girl looked him in the eye and asked, "Will you be my friend?" He squawked again and flew off.

She thought to herself, *I'm all alone now*.

One
First Look

The dramatic wrap-around veranda of Le Grande Manor showcased the three-story antebellum. Solidly built and spacious, the front door transom and sidelights made for a bright and welcoming entry to the 1834 home. The wood construction for the earlier generations of the Le Grande family assured the family that the home would stand forever. Over several generations, the house had worn many coats of pale-yellow paint, and great care had been taken to preserve the integrity of the wood siding. Dark brown side shutters framed each of the windows, and those on the first floor gave the impression of open arms upon approach to the front door. A tin roof covered the structure and on stormy days, the raindrops played a unique melody pinging off the roof.

The 200-acre estate was located in the countryside outside of Atlanta, Georgia; tall trees grew close together, creating a protective thicket around the perimeter of the property. A rolling lawn, a huge driveway that circled a beautiful magnolia tree sprouted blossoms the size of dinner plates, framed the majestic house standing as a testament to the endurance of the Le Grande family.

Honeysuckle and jasmine climbed up the sides of the low railing on the veranda and left their sweet aroma in the air with each delicate breeze that blew through the vines.

A perfectly laid out and maintained herb and vegetable garden sat on the south side of the house yielding hearty tomatoes, green beans, okra, Brussels sprouts, basil, chives, dill, green onions, and parsley. Impatiens in purples and pink, bright red geraniums, begonias, purple and white pansies and petunias created a breathtaking picture against the yellow background of the house. Massive mounds of white and purple alyssum filled the space in between the St. John's Wort and snowball hydrangeas. A long bed of lavender plants ran the full length of one side of the house, their magnificent stalks waving, "Hel-lo? Hey y'all," to passersby.

Later, the heavenly-scented blossoms would be dried and used in sachet packets or placed in crystal vases atop antique tables.

Original hitching posts still stood at attention alongside the driveway where, in times gone by, horses were tied when visitors came to call. One could almost picture beautiful women alighting from carriages pulled by big, white horses. The old *carriage house that stood fifty feet or so behind the main house had become nearly obscured by kudzu, one of those pesky vines that grew wild in that part of the South. Now a converted garage, it housed a fairly new automobile.*

The room used most often was the kitchen. It had been redecorated reflecting the era of the fifties, with bright yellow cabinets, red Formica countertops, and black-and-white checkerboard linoleum flooring. A yellow stove located across from the yellow refrigerator added to the cheery room. Café curtains with a pattern of brightly colored teapots hung over the windows above the sink and in the breakfast area.

The room now aged into dreariness, with its faded curtains and well-worn linoleum; the once cheery appliances, although well taken care of, had faded. There was a history there, and to disrupt that with new things was not a part of any future plans.

Chloe, sitting in a glider on the side porch, watched the rain and talked on her cell phone to a friend. She twirled her long blonde hair between her fingers, and subconsciously crossed and uncrossed her legs during the conversation. She sighed, "I hate being here, stuck out in the middle of nowhere in the 19th century! I'm surprised I even got through to you. I'll have to talk fast because cell reception out here is almost non-existent. There is nothing to do here on

15

'Planet Nowhere', the rain is coming down in buckets, and I'm missing the biggest party of the year."

"Hey, chill, girl. It's only for two weeks."

"That's easy for you to say. You're there in total civilization with tv and a computer, and I'm like, stranded. This is so lame! Why did my parents think it would be good for me to get to know my grandma, especially during the most important two weeks of the summer? I haven't seen my grandma since I was four. What? Almost eight years ago! Being sent here is like a prison sentence. You should have seen the fit I threw at the airport."

"Weren't your parents angry with you?"

"I didn't care that people stared at us. I'd rather be anywhere but here. My life, as I knew it, is over."

Silence was all she heard. "Becky? Say something." She moved to try to pick up the signal and absentmindedly walked out into the rain. "Oh, great!" She growled in frustration, stormed into the house, and slammed the door behind her.

Chloe was an only child and had looked forward to spending the summer hanging out with her other popular friends.

Her grandma, Crystal, stood at the kitchen counter. Her bright blue eyes remained partially hidden behind glasses perched on the end of her nose as she read a recipe. Her once-blonde hair was tied back in a bun. She used the back of one hand to push back a wisp now streaked with gray, from her forehead. When the door slammed, she called out, "Chloe, please don't slam the door."

"Whatever," she responded, making a face. "What's for dinner?"

Without looking up, Grandma smiled. "My special chicken cordon bleu."

Chloe spun on her heel and glared at her grandma. "I hate chicken. Why don't you ever make a nice risotto? It wouldn't hurt you, you know."

Grandma removed her glasses, turned to the sink, and rinsed her hands. She dried them on a towel and turned. "What a mess you've made, Chloe. Look at the mud you've tracked all over the kitchen floor. I thought you were more responsible than that. In my day, we would never have thought of being so careless, or speak to our elders as you have. I swear that girls nowadays are no better than boys. They're all slobs. I know you were taught better than that." Grandma wiped her eyes with the corner of her apron, as she stepped away from her granddaughter.

Chloe half-heartedly began to clean up the mess on the floor and grumbled, "In my day," mimicking her grandma's words, but her grandma waved her off.

"Just leave."

Chloe turned to leave but tracked more mud with her shoes. Grandma shook her head and leaned against the counter.

"This sure isn't the way I wanted our visit to begin. Please take off your shoes and put them in the mudroom."

Chloe rolled her eyes, and as she walked toward the mudroom, she turned to her grandma and blasted out in a very nasty voice, "I can't wait for these two weeks to be over. I'm sick of the rules and being in this stupid old house, and I'm sick of you!"

Grandma didn't reply as Chloe stormed out. Disappointed, she asked herself, *was I ever like that*? Chloe continued to pout as she removed her shoes and half-heartedly cleaned off the mud with a piece of paper towel. She glanced around and wondered where she could put them, so she wouldn't be yelled at again. She plopped them down next to other shoes that had been set to dry on a shelf and stomped out of the room. She grabbed her cell phone from her pocket to call her friend, saw that the signal now blinked only one bar, and angrily shoved it back into her pant pocket as she climbed the staircase to the second floor. In front of her was the stairway leading to the forbidden attic; the one that Grandma had prohibited her to explore. NO arguing allowed. Period!

She wondered, *why didn't the old lady want me in there? She isn't going to tell me what to do. I'll show her*! She went to the door and jiggled the door handle. *Darn! It's locked.*

Two
Into the Attic

Chloe crept close to the wall of the hallway outside of the kitchen and spied on her grandma in the kitchen. She was sitting on a stool, holding her head in her hands as if she were asleep, but Chloe knew better. They had yelled at one another, and her grandma was hurt.

Too bad, Chloe thought, *as if she never did anything wrong! What makes her think she's so perfect? What gives her the right to boss me around?*

As she walked past the kitchen and out onto the back porch, Chloe pulled out her cell phone to find a stronger signal there and punched in a number. The house phone rang. From her vantage point, Chloe peered around the corner and watched as her grandma slowly rose from the stool and entered the parlor to answer it.

Chloe heard her say, "Hello? Hello?" Satisfied that she had enough time, she ran to the kitchen, rifled through a drawer and found an old key on a ring, which she stuffed into the right front pocket of her jeans. With a smirk of triumph on her face, she ran out of the kitchen but left the drawer slightly ajar.

Grandma shook her head as she re-entered the kitchen. "Wrong number I guess." Then she noticed the partially open drawer and absentmindedly shut it completely. She looked around the kitchen and tried to refocus on finishing the preparation of dinner, but her heart wasn't in it.

She had always served chicken cordon bleu to her family for special occasions, and Chloe's outburst had put a damper on any enthusiasm she may have had to continue. *What did I do wrong? Why was Chloe so angry? Doesn't she know how much this visit means to both of us*? Chloe obviously didn't care, and that hurt even more.

As Chloe walked up the stairway from the first floor to the landing, she noticed a stained-glass window she had not previously recalled seeing. The light shined through a field of colorful glass flowers in the wooden frame. She continued to the second floor until she was back at the base of the stairs to the attic. Chloe looked around to see whether her grandma had followed her, and once she was sure that she was alone she slowly climbed the sixteen steps to the top. Not realizing that she was doing so, she found herself counting the steps and thought, *that's weird*. Taking the key from her jeans' pocket, she inserted it and turned it with great difficulty. She feared for a minute that she had taken the wrong key, and knowing that if that were true, she wouldn't be able to pull the same phone trick to search again. *Okay, key, do your thing.* With another try, the lock clicked, and she turned the knob. "Yes!" The door swung open, and with a deep breath, Chloe took a step into the attic.

The room had a high-pitched ceiling with exposed rafter beams. As Chloe turned her head and looked at the highest peak, she noticed colored light gently streaming into the room. Its origin was from a stained-glass window very high on one of the walls. She slowly turned around and stepped back to see more of the window and ran into a spider web. Giving out a low squeal, she quickly covered her mouth in hopes that she hadn't been detected and wiped away the silky web remains—"Yuk"— as she brushed away more tiny pieces. She swore she heard someone laugh, but quickly dismissed that notion.

The sound of the rain magnified itself in the attic. In the distance, lightning illuminated the sky, and the clap of thunder made her jump. On one of the walls, a small partially-open window allowed a gentle breeze to blow through which helped a little to keep the room cool, considering that it was another hot and humid summer. Some raindrops landed on the windowsill and puddled on its surface. The water ran down the wall and followed the same path caused by previous rains.

As Chloe looked around, she noticed an old potbellied stove, one or two rolled up pieces of carpet, a pile of old books, some old lamps without shades, a couple of faded paintings stacked against a wall, and a pair of snow skis (one broken) secured by an old rope, hanging from a couple of beams. It dawned on Chloe that her mouth was wide open as she took it all in. "Cool!"

Another clap of thunder sounded, and Chloe shivered as chills ran down her spine. She heard music in the distance that sounded like it came from a radio in the kitchen below. A breeze moved her hair, and she dismissed it as coming from the window.

She began to search around the room and found an old hat perched atop a piece of furniture that looked like a cross between an old three-legged milking stool and an end table. Chloe tried on the hat, twirled around like a model, and looked around in vain for a mirror, or something shiny so she could see herself. She cautiously moved things around. Behind some boxes, she spied an old wind-up phonograph. She remembered seeing one just like it in an old black-and-white movie on TV one night while she channel-surfed. Speaking to no one in particular, she said, "Maybe there are old records up here, too." She lifted the top of the phonograph and found a record on the turntable. "Awesome."

The handle stuck out of the side of the phonograph, and with some difficulty she cranked it up. She moved the arm down onto the record, and all she heard was a scratching sound. When she raised the underside of the arm, she saw that it held no needle. "Shoot!"

Still anxious to find something that would be the reason her grandmother didn't want her up there, she saw an old trunk. Chloe knew she was invading someone's space, but she lifted the lid anyway. Several journals, a photo album, and a piece of paper that looked like a map, lay on top. Chloe put it all back in the trunk lid and picked up one of the journals. There was a title on the front, *The Enchanted Carousel,1951.*

"Okay, let's see what this is," Chloe commented to no one in particular, as she sat down on the floor and leaned against the trunk. Instead of reading from the beginning, she cracked the book open at random and began to read:

I was a tiny baby, with big blue eyes, and blonde curly hair. My nursery was decorated with carousel horses and bright colors.

"I think I'm going to hurl!" Chloe remarked, but continued to skim over the paragraphs.

The baby curls are gone, never to return. I am going to be tall like my father, and slim like my mom – jeans are my favorite piece of clothing. Bugs and snakes didn't scare me – I treasure the time we spent together—

"Lame, lame, lame-o! Sounds like something from Anne of Green Gables. How very *sweeeeeet*," was her facetious remark, as she continued to read.

My dream was to have my own horse to love – My parents gave me a carousel rocking horse for my third Christmas – my grandmother told me that if I continued to believe, one day I would have my horse – I believe, I believe.

Chloe found she was totally bored and continued to skip around. "Yawn. I guess the fifties really were dull." She turned to another page, and read the first few words aloud:

I had a huge emptiness in my heart after this tremendous loss. Grandmother was to have custody of me, and after my folks died, I went to live with her. I didn't want to leave my friends, my school, and the only home I had ever known. I would be stuck out in the sticks, away from civilization —

Chloe sighed. "Sounds familiar. I wonder if she was as bored as I am." Even though she thought the entry was dribble, she couldn't put it down. She flipped a few pages ahead and read the beginning of the next chapter in the journal.

One rainy afternoon, I was very bored.

"A-ha!" was Chloe's remark, and then began reading the page again.

One rainy afternoon, I was very bored. I had lived with Grandmother Bertie for almost a year, and

24

had been in every part of her house except the attic. Since the house was a couple of hundred years old, parts of it were not in the best condition. The attic was off-limits because of the danger of falling through the old floor. Well, since I considered myself grown up, I decided the rules didn't apply to me.

I knew where Grandmother hid the keys, and with a little twinge of guilt I checked to be sure she wasn't around, slipped into the pantry and removed the keys from a peg on the wall behind some jars of homemade jam. I carefully closed the door to the pantry and began an adventure I could never have imagined.

My intention was not to be malicious; I just thought that this was a good way for me to spend an afternoon. I don't know if you have ever seen the contents of an attic in an old Southern home, but I can tell you that it is awesome.

Chloe abruptly stopped reading after that paragraph and uttered a half-hearted laugh. Something had struck a familiar chord. *Who is this girl?* She paused, and turned to the front of the journal again and read the handwritten title on the inside page. *The Enchanted Carousel, 1951, by Crystal Baxter.* "Ohmigod! That's Grandma," she exclaimed. Chloe sat back against the trunk, stunned, and flipped the pages back to the beginning of the journal and once again began to read, taking a trip back in time.

She had the feeling that she was not alone in the attic but continued to ignore it. Could this be true, or was the guilt of disobeying her grandmother making her feel that way? She leaned back and closed her eyes for just a moment and felt someone or something touch her shoulder. A startled Chloe opened her eyes to see a flicker of an image pass her on its way toward the far corner of the room. She felt differently somehow, like being outside of her body, watching everything from afar. *What is going on? What, or who, was that? That's very strange.*

She was still sitting on the cushion with the journal spread out on her lap as the music intensified. Chloe felt herself swallowed up in the past, as if she were being swept over a waterfall, and became part of the story.

Three
Crystal's Journal Begins

"Once upon a time," my grandmother said, with a twinkle in her eye. This was always the way she began her bedtime stories to me when I was just a little girl. I was born Crystal Elizabeth Baxter, the only child of Margaret and Carter Baxter. My parents were devoted to me and were very sad they could never give me a brother or sister. I was a tiny baby, with big blue eyes, and blonde curly hair. Most of the pictures I have seen show that my hair was dark when I was born, sticking out all over the place. It began to turn 'golden blonde' when I was about six months old. I was a good child, always smiling and hardly ever cried. That is, if you can believe my grandmother.

My nursery was decorated with carousel horses and bright colors. No bears or other animals, just horses. The wallpaper had a border running all around the room with paintings of carousel horses. They looked like they were moving in a circle. My grandmother told me I was fascinated by the horses swirling around on tiny strings attached to the carousel mobile over my crib. I would spend hours singing my baby songs to the music of the mobile and clapping my hands in glee. I was only about ten months old, but my love for the beautiful horses was growing.

When it came time to give gifts, friends and family selected horses and carousels. My room was filled with them. On shelves were music boxes, statues, stuffed animals. All horses and carousels. My favorite snuggly toy was a stuffed horse, instead of a teddy bear. I would learn later on why I had that love and attraction to carousels and horses.

Grandmother said, "You learned to walk rather quickly once you got the knack of it. I figured you had lots to do and places to go and wanted to waste no time in getting there. You walked on your toes, and your family was sure you would become a ballerina one day. You would raise your little hands above your head and twirl around and around.

"We all had to keep a close eye on you, because you seemed to have one walking speed – fast. It was quite a chore to keep up with you. The only thing that made you stop was when I told you I was going to tell you a story about a little girl and an enchanted carousel. Instantly, you climbed up into my lap and waited while I began my story. Before I could finish, you would be asleep, dreaming of horses and carousels." I can hear Grandmother's words even now.

By the time I was two, my hair was halfway down my back. Mother used to sit me on a stool in front of her and brush my curls around her finger with a natural bristle brush. I didn't mind, but it was sometimes hard to sit still that long. My hair had some natural curl, and the ceremony of brushing helped. When the weather was humid, there was no controlling what my hair would do. The baby curls are gone, never to return. That's why I wear a ponytail most of the time. There is one piece of hair with a mind of its own, refusing to stay in the rubber band. I find myself twirling it when I am concentrating or nervous.

I was a tomboy, and when I was about three, my dad took me fishing and hiking and exploring. We loved to camp out, and bugs and snakes didn't scare me, much to his delight. I treasure the time we spent together.

Grandmother was still a relatively young woman when I was born, admitting to being fifty-five, however no one really knew for sure. She was responsible for giving me the name, Crystal. According to stories repeated within my family, my Great-Grandmother Eunice, who was my Grandmother Bertie's mother, had a fertile imagination to the point that the rest of the family believed her to be a little 'off'.

Grandmother said, "My mother knew how to

make amazing things happen by saying a few special words and 'believing'."

"Well," I thought, "was that really true or another one of her stories?"

Temporarily shaken back to the present, Chloe shivered again and tried to get up but found that either her leg had gone to sleep, or something was holding her down. "Who is there? Show yourself! I don't like this game-playing, and I am not afraid of you, whoever you are." Chloe tried to sound brave, but underneath her veneer, she remained uneasy about being in the forbidden attic and prying into her grandma's private journal.

How else was she going to find out about her life? Part of her didn't care, but deep down she really wanted to know. When it appeared that she was alone, Chloe shook her leg to wake it up, twirled a piece of hair that had fallen out from under her hat, and promptly fell back into the nineteenth century.

On the day I was christened, Grandmother Bertie gave me a tiny crystal horse that hung on a gold chain. I was too small to wear it then and kept it in a jewelry box until I was eight, when Grandmother put it around my neck and said, "It has been in the family for years to be passed on to a daughter or granddaughter every other generation. This is now

30

your generation."

I wear it all of the time. Anytime I'm afraid or not sure of something, I rub the crystal horse until it becomes warm and makes me calm. I never figured out what special thing happened that gave me that peace.

From time to time throughout my childhood, my parents had to go away on business trips, and I always stayed with Grandmother Bertie. I looked forward to the "Once Upon a Time" stories she told me every night at bedtime. Her mother had given her a beautiful crystal pendant, which she wore on a velvet ribbon around her neck. She subconsciously rubbed it as she repeated the stories that I had heard hundreds of times. She made all of the stories come alive. As unbelievable as they were, Bertie swore they were true. Grandmother told me that she had special insight, abilities to see into the future, and if I had a special wish or dream, it would come true if I believed. I secretly wished I had those special abilities.

I always managed to fall asleep before she finished, but somehow the stories crept into my dreams. At night when the wind blew, I heard the sound of a calliope sending its lilting music through the trees.

Returning to reality, Chloe looked up as the music she

31

had heard before drifted through the window. It sounded like calliope music, like she remembered hearing when she had ridden the carousel at Disney World. Where was it coming from? *It's my imagination, because I'm so hooked on the diary right now.* She returned to the story.

Since I had a very fertile imagination, I sometimes found it difficult to separate fantasy from reality, but I never felt I was too old for Grandmother's stories. Of course, I would never share that secret with my friends. They already believed I was a little strange.

I dreamed that someday I would own a horse to love. I prayed every night, asking God to send me one. Ever since I can remember, probably from the equine mobile over my crib, I have loved carousels and horses. My grandmother told me that if I continued to believe, one day I would have my horse. 'I believe, I believe.' I rubbed the charm and prayed that somehow my wish would come true.

One Christmas when I was about four, I received a huge package from my parents. Inside was a one-half scale carousel rocking horse, complete with a brass pole for me to hold onto. I squealed with excitement, "My horse. My horse." I had determined that this would be my horse until the real thing came along. I spent many happy hours sitting in the saddle and fantasizing about riding off to faraway places. I still have that rocking horse, but now it sits in the corner of my room, my pride and joy and a memory of happy days as a small child.

I imagined myself in Grandmother Bertie's stories, always the heroine riding off on a white stallion. While my friends thought me weird, it was a special treat for them to ride on my rocking horse. At other times, while they were playing with their dolls, I only dreamed about tomboy things. It has always been a mystery to me why girls think they have to be afraid of bugs and worms and stuff like that. As I got older, I gathered everything I could about my passion.

Being a bit of a loner, probably because I was an only child, and on the occasions my parents were out of the country, I had a lot of time to devote to things I considered really important, like putting together a scrapbook filled with clippings and pictures of horses.

Grandmother helped me cut out the pictures, and since I had been taught how to use the scissors and paste, I spent a lot of time alone and worked on this labor of love.

Chloe was intrigued with her grandma's descriptions of how to create a scrapbook. *I don't have anything that means that much to me. Why is that? Grandma was an only child, but seemed to be very well-adjusted,* she mused.

Most memories of my childhood are very foggy. I can remember some things clearly, and then my mind blanks out. There are some incidents I would like to erase, like the day when I was eleven-years-old and got lost on my way home from school. I was day-dreaming about horses no doubt, and not paying attention to my path, and wound up in a cemetery. I wasn't very far from Grandmother Bertie's house, but I wandered around totally lost. In the distance, I heard calliope music just as I did at night sometimes. It scared me as darkness approached, and I could hardly breathe. "Dear God, please help me." I sat on a cold, marble bench; tried to swallow and shook. I rubbed the crystal horse until it was so hot I couldn't hold onto it and cried out for my mother. I was so afraid I would never see my family again, and coincidentally, that was the same day my parents died in an automobile accident. I was very angry at God for letting this happen. What possible reason could there be for taking the two most important people in my life? Now, I was really alone and scared more than I had ever been before.

Chloe stopped reading for a minute. *I didn't know that Grandma's parents were killed. How awful! She was just my age.* She turned her eyes back to the handwriting on the page, which was different from the previous entries. It seemed like she had taken great care with each word, as if she were writing a letter to God, and yet the final words were shaky, like maybe she had been crying when she wrote them.

Chloe was quite moved by what she had just read. Although she and her parents didn't always get along, she would hate to lose them. How had her grandma coped with that? Her eyes drifted to the next page in the journal, her boredom moving to a stronger interest in knowing what secrets were hidden within those pages.

Should I be reading this? The journal is full of Grandma's private thoughts. Are there things in there that should best be forgotten, or maybe because it happened so long ago, and Grandma is so old, it just may not matter now? I'll just read a few more pages.

Once again, she felt something touch her shoulder, and she was transported into the story as if she were there and seeing everything she was reading and hearing her grandma's voice, as she read on.

Four
Bertha and Le Grande Manor

There was a huge emptiness in my heart after this tragedy. I didn't want to be selfish, because after all, my grandmother had lost her daughter. We sometimes are so caught up in our own grief, we tend to forget about others who are left behind. I held on to my crystal horse, knowing that somehow everything would be all right. According to my parents' will, my Grandmother Bertie was to have custody of me, so after my folks died, I went to live with her. Even though I loved my grandmother very much, I didn't want to leave my friends, my school, and the only home I had ever known.

Grandmother Bertha Louise Becket is my grandmother on my mother's side of the family. Her maiden name was Le Grande – a very strong name. I think she was very beautiful in her younger years, and she still has the grace of a Southern lady. She lives in Georgia, where she was born and raised, married, and had two children – my mother and my uncle. My grandfather died when I was very young, and I don't really remember him, but I could see from pictures that he was a handsome man; a good catch, as they say.

I am so grateful now to be with my grandmother, even though I was very angry and disappointed at first. We come from different generations and have had disagreements from time to time. I love her, and it is not her fault that she is stuck with me, but she can be so square sometimes!

Still a part of the past, Chloe was amazed at how much her grandma's feelings and thoughts paralleled her own. She had not wanted to be away from her friends either, but Grandma seemed to adjust a lot better than she was doing. *She was an only child just like me but seemed to have a good relationship with her parents. And she was away from them a lot. She must have hated that. I love my parents, but they make me so mad sometimes.*

My friends didn't make the move any easier, because they said they would never see me again, and I would be stuck out in the sticks, away from civilization. The first couple of months I was with her I was miserable, angry, and threatened to run away. She suggested that she run away with me, since we were both suffering the same loss. How was I ever going to get along with someone so much older than me? I did not understand her life, and she certainly didn't

37

understand mine.

Out loud, Chloe observed, "Maybe we have more in common than I thought."

Grandmother Bertie (she preferred that name to Bertha) lives on a big estate, called Le Grande Manor, in the country outside of Atlanta, Georgia. The house is huge and so is all of the property it sits on. Lots of trees and flowers are planted all over the place. There are still 'hitching posts' alongside the driveway, where horses were tied when visitors came to call. In my mind, I could see carriages pulled by white horses. Inside the carriages were beautiful ladies dressed up in long gowns. There were stables for the horses and a carriage house to store them. Now, Grandmother parks her car there.

She had everything from my room brought to her home at Le Grande Manor. At least I had my favorite things around me, including my rocking horse and other treasures. That helped make the move easier, but I still cried every night. I could hear Grandmother sobbing in her room, too, and I crept into her room and snuggled closely to her. I knew she was not in the mood for 'Once upon a time' stories, and we soon fell asleep.

Le Grande Manor has been in the family for over four generations. It is full of great nooks and niches, and the stairs creak when you walk on them. The kitchen is huge and has been recently redecorated with bright yellow cabinets, red Formica countertops, and black-and-white checkerboard linoleum flooring. Grandmother keeps it shiny by waxing it every week. Multi-colored pots hang above the sink and yellow stove, which sits across from the yellow refrigerator. It is a very cheerful room. Grandmother made some pretty curtains with a pattern of teapots on them that she hung at the windows over the sink and in the breakfast area. I love the kitchen; it is very comfortable. The bathrooms have also been modernized. I am glad about that because generations ago they didn't have inside plumbing.

Grandmother inherited the old homestead and has lovingly added her personality into the decorating. She told me, "A home should be comfortable, allowing its residents to feel like they were putting on a pair of old slippers when they entered."

Children and animals are more than welcome, and the vases are always filled with all kinds of flowers. It doesn't matter what time of the year; Grandmother Bertie can make things grow. I think she must possess some of the special abilities she talks about in her stories.

Her mother and father (my great-grandparents)

moved to this beautiful spot shortly after they were married in 1855. My great-great-grandfather's family built the house in 1834 and raised six children here. With a standing seam (a tin) roof and a great veranda that runs around three sides of the house on the main level, it is like so many homes of that era. On the south side of the porch, Grandmother has placed white wicker chairs, topped with big, soft cushions the color of freshly churned butter. Several colorful pots sit proudly on wrought iron stands, filled to overflowing with huge, fragrant blossoms, green ivy and tiny white flowers. The aroma is wonderful.

On rainy days, you can hear the 'ping, ping' of the raindrops playing a melody on the tin roof. Very often, I hear the familiar calliope music, but still don't know why or where it is coming from. My favorite thing to do is to sit and glide back and forth in the big, oversized swing that sits next to the wicker chairs, reading or adding pictures to my scrapbook. Sometimes I fall asleep and dream about magical things. Did I have the same imagination my Great-Grandmother Eunice had, or is it just a plot from one of Grandmother Bertie's stories?

I am, at this writing, twelve years old, just having had my birthday. I like to write, probably because of my mom. She told me, "It is good to write down experiences, so we can look back and enjoy or learn from them."

It looks like I am going to be tall like my father and slim like my mom. I am not very graceful, much to my grandmother's dismay. It must be that awkward stage grownups talk about. Frankly, I think my nose is too big, but Grandmother says I have 'royal features'. My hair never behaves, flying all over the place, especially when the weather is humid. The baby curls are gone, never to return. That's why I wear a ponytail most of the time. There is one piece of hair with a mind of its own, refusing to stay in the rubber band. I find myself twirling it when I am concentrating or nervous; a habit I am really trying to quit.

I still have large blue eyes and long eyelashes, so I guess God did have a sense of compassion after all. I am very strong – a real tomboy. I love to climb trees, swim, and explore. Jeans are my favorite piece of clothing. My favorite pair of shoes is bare feet!

Living out in the 'sticks' has not been all bad, actually. I ride my bicycle to school every day and sometimes stop at a friend's house to listen to music or do homework. I find myself comparing their parents to mine – I know that is a bad thing to do, but I miss them so much. My grandmother told me, "Never come home late, because that will worry me, and the one thing I know that you don't want to do is to worry anyone." I have my chores to do once I get home and try very hard to get everything finished

41

before dinner. Sometimes my friends come for a sleepover – at least, the ones who are not afraid of bugs and stuff like that. Some of my girlfriends have really taken to digging around in the dirt looking for night crawlers so we can go fishing. I never thought I would see that!

Grandmother has made a huge impression on me, and I want to be just like her when I grow up. She says that there is time, and I know one day that I will make her proud. I learned from her how to knit and crochet and cook; skills that most young girls are not taught these days. When I was still very young, maybe eight, on occasions when I stayed with Grandmother, my girlfriends from the city used to come to my house, and we played 'make-believe'. I always chose names for them during our tea parties and pretended we were really grown up in our own little world. The only things I didn't let my friends play with was my carousel collection – music boxes, miniatures, some carved from wood, others made of blown glass or plastic. I was particular about my carousel collection. That was totally off-limits.

I love school and have never had a difficult time in that area. It must be my passion to learn all about everything, I guess. Figuring out numbers and puzzles is fascinating. Perhaps that is why I was chosen to – but I am getting ahead of my story.

Five
Sixteen Steps

One rainy afternoon, I was very bored. I had lived with Grandmother Bertie for almost a year and had been in every part of her house, except the attic. Since the house was over a hundred years old, I guessed that parts of it were not in the best condition.

One day shortly after moving in with her, she told me, "The attic is off-limits because of the danger of falling through the old floor. I don't want you up there."

Well, since I considered myself grown up, I decided the rules didn't apply to me. I knew where she hid the keys, and with a little twinge of guilt, I checked to be sure she wasn't around, slipped into the pantry and removed the keys from a peg on the wall behind jars of homemade jam. I carefully closed the door to the pantry and began an adventure I could never have imagined. My intention was not to be malicious; I just thought that was a good way for me to spend an afternoon. I don't know if you have ever seen the contents of an attic in an old Southern home, but I can tell you that it is pretty amazing.

43

Chloe yelled out, "She did the same thing I did! Go, Grandma."

I climbed the sixteen creaky steps (I always count the number of steps), up to what I was sure would be a room full of tattered old clothes and rusty lamps and the like. A feeling of excitement came over me. I cannot explain what the feeling was, but as I approached the last of the steps, my heart began to beat rapidly, and I felt dizzy with anticipation. I found myself clutching the crystal horse hanging around my neck, praying I would not fall through the old floor. In the distance, I heard the calliope music again and almost turned around and went back. My curiosity got the better of me, and I continued.

Chloe was amazed at the fact that her grandmother had also counted the steps. She felt herself right alongside her grandma as she began her journey, her mind taking her back in time.

What lay before me was a large room, full of neatly stacked boxes and trunks, and several what appeared to be dress mannequins, wearing the most beautiful gowns I had ever seen, except in museums and the movies. As I moved closer, I could actually see the lovely women who once wore those dresses. They were smiling at me, curtsying, and the sound of the calliope once again filled my ears. Of course, I was sure my eyes were playing tricks on me, so I blinked, and the faces and forms of the ladies disappeared. I called out, "Please don't go away. Come back." As I shook my head, and cautiously made my way around the room, I sensed the presence of someone in the room with me but dismissed that as being my imagination – again. I tried to find the source of the music and discovered that a black raven sitting on the sill in the partially open window was watching me.

"Hell-o," I said. He looked like the same raven that came to me the day of the funeral. "I'm not afraid of you. In fact, I hope that you will stay around and keep me company."

He was flapping his wings and shaking his head, and in his beak, he was holding a golden ring. Seemingly on purpose, he dropped the ring which rolled to my feet. Naturally, I was startled, let out a loud gasp, and the raven flew away, his huge wings making a whooshing sound as he left. The ring was heavy and tarnished with age. Since it was too large to wear on my finger and too small to wear on my wrist, I slipped it onto my crystal horse necklace. He must have wanted me to do something, but since there was a lot more to explore, I decided to continue my quest.

Have you ever been somewhere, a certain aroma

fills the space, and it takes you back to another time? I felt very close to something or someone but could not put my finger on what it was. I swore I saw a young girl in a floppy hat, holding a large gardenia, sitting on one of the rafters, and I called out, "What are you doing up there? Is that your flower I smell? It is very nice. Why don't you come down here and talk to me?" She disappeared, but I could still smell the gardenia.

The scent of gardenias suddenly filled the attic, and as Chloe turned around, she saw what appeared to be a figure wearing a hat, drifting up toward the rafters. *Yeah, sure. I am simply re-living my grandma's visions. Ghosts aren't real.*

Chloe felt herself slipping over the waterfall again, sharing her grandma's experience in the attic.

I was a bit surprised by the girl but did not intend for her to deter me. I wondered aloud, "Where shall I begin my treasure hunt?" I recalled the stories about my great-grandmother and her ability to make things happen if she just believed. So, laughing to myself, I thought I would call on her to show me around. "Okay, GG"—for Great-Grandmother—"where do I begin?" The thought was no sooner out of my head than one of the trunks moved away from the others. I jumped back, sure that once again, my eyes were playing tricks on me.

A slight glow formed around the lid of the trunk, and I approached very cautiously, my mind in a sort of haze.

I felt as though I was dreaming; that maybe I had fallen asleep, and I was in one of Grandmother Bertie's stories. I reached out to touch the top of the trunk. As soon as my fingers touched the lid, it flew open, revealing a photo album and several old journals. My heart jumped up into my throat, and I tried to swallow it down to where it belonged. In a few seconds, I was ready to go on.

I remembered my mother telling me that her grandparents used to write down everything in a journal – where they had gone, things about the family – so that future generations would be able to read about their ancestors. It was like a diary but didn't appear to have been written in every day – only when they thought it was important and not to be forgotten. There were some dates, however. The handwriting was beautiful. Inside the back cover of the journal was an old curling piece of paper on which was drawn what looked like a treasure map. I elected not to begin reading the journals at this time, since there were so many other things to see.

I cautiously picked up the photo album. "Okay, so far, so good. I haven't been shocked or anything, so I figure it is all right to continue." Clearly, I could see that it was covered with real leather, embossed with gold lettering which I could not make out because it had been worn down with age. A narrow, leather strap surrounded the book and kept the pages secure. I found a large, soft cushion on top of a low stool, and with my 'treasure' in my arms, I settled into the cushion and slowly, but carefully, untied the leather strap, and allowed the cover of the album to open and expose the pages.

When the book opened, I began a journey into my ancestors' lives. There, on the pages of this old photo album, were pictures of generations of my family. Can these be the heroes from Grandmother Bertie's stories? Each of the photos was labeled, with a short description of who the people were, the year the picture was taken, and so forth. As I turned each page, drinking in the amazing history in front of me, I realized that the dresses that adorned the mannequins were identical to those worn by the women in the pictures, and the faces I had seen on the mannequins were theirs! I had never seen these pictures of my great-grandmother and the other ladies, until that moment. I looked around the room but the 'visions' I had seen were no longer there.

Chloe shook her head, brought herself back to reality, and said to no one in particular, "This is totally awesome." She looked around the attic, secretly hoping that she would encounter the same visions that her grandma had, so many years ago. Feeling confident that the girl in the hat was no longer around, Chloe put the journal down for a few minutes and hunted around to see if she could find the mannequins. She pulled back an old tri-fold screen and found them. They were covered with sheets, and as she pulled back the first one, she saw the same beautiful gowns. "Have they been here all of these years? Wouldn't they have been in bad shape, instead of looking so fresh? What is going on here?" She was talking aloud again, but the excitement was quite intense. The mannequins had no faces and did not curtsy, but she still understood how her grandmother must have felt when she encountered the vision fifty years before.

"Cool." She gently arranged the mannequins around her, so she would have company since she was not able to share this experience with anyone. A chill ran through her body, and she was not sure she wasn't dreaming. She did smell the gardenias again, though. Chloe picked up the journal and once again stepped back into her grandma's story.

Many pages were devoted to pictures of the house and grounds. There were beautiful gardens, a stable, and in one of the pictures, way in the background, I saw what appeared to be a carousel enclosure. It looked like a different piece of property because I did not see the big house; just the pavilion and a small shack nearby. As was the custom in those days, many wealthy families purchased a merry-go-round for their children and housed it in a structure that would protect it from the elements in bad weather. "I'm sure my imagination is in overdrive – maybe I'm dreaming." I had explored the property, I thought, and I did not remember ever seeing it before. I looked at the picture again, and there it was, as plain as day. At that moment, I thought, 'Now I know why I love carousels and horses. It's in my blood.'

As I read the labels, I discovered that my GG had five sisters who had all been born in Georgia, in this very house. I could see a familiarity in those lovely faces to my own beautiful mother and grandmother. It seemed as if they were reaching out to me – like they had some special secret to share. As I continued through the photo album, I felt transported back to a different time; back to my great-grandmother's time. I was no longer a young girl living in the 1950s, but in the mid-1800s. Everything my grandmother had told me about believing was right there!

At that time, the presence I had felt upon entering the room was stronger, and as I turned around, I saw a young girl about my age. However, this girl was not the same one who wore the hat. This one was dressed in white, and I could see through her. Aw, come on, what's that all about? Her hair was a beautiful golden blond, tied back with a satin ribbon. Her skin was like fine porcelain, and she was tall and slim. Although I could see through her at first, she seemed to fade in and out, the longer she remained. Afraid to close my eyes, and more afraid not to, I sat there on the cushion, willing her away. But she didn't go. Instead, she came and stood in front of me, and spoke very softly. Her voice was like a beautiful melody.

"Crystal, I am so happy that you are finally here. I have waited for over fifty years for you. I do not want you to be afraid, but I do need you to listen to what I have to say. When I died, I should have crossed over and been reunited with my father, who died shortly after I did. I think I know how my accident happened, but I do not know for sure. Some force is keeping us from reuniting, and I can't cross over to be with him and my mother. I have chosen you to solve a mystery that has been in the family for generations. I need to be set free, and you are the only one who can help me. You only have two weeks to complete it, the date which would have been my twelfth birthday." Her final words were, "Please, I beg of you, help me. If you do not, I will have to wait two more generations. Find the Carousel."

"Wait a minute," I called out to her. "My birthday is also in two weeks! Who are you? Why do you need to be free? Free from what, or who? What

is the mystery that you spoke about? Who is keeping you from crossing over? What about the carousel? Please come back and talk to me again." Then she faded away, and I never saw her again. Was this all really happening, or had I been dreaming? Off in the distance, the calliope music grew louder, and I heard a young, female voice crying. I don't think it was the young girl, because the sound was not soft like hers. I held tightly to my crystal horse.

"What kind of twilight zone is this?" Chloe totally freaked out. She looked at the mannequins again to see if they had faces now. "Are you ghosts, too? Are there more ghosts up here? OMG, what have I fallen into? No wonder the attic was off-limits."

"Seriously, there are no such things as ghosts; there are no such things as ghosts. These mannequins are just that – no faces, no curtsying. I figure I can do one of two things; go downstairs and apologize to Grandma for disobeying her, or continue reading her journal, which really is probably just one more of her stories." What exactly did she hear? It was the sound of someone crying in the distance. "This can't be happening." Chloe reopened the journal, her decision made, she digressed into the past.

I quickly closed the album, replaced the leather strap, picked up the journals, shook my head, took a deep breath, and before I left, looked around the room. I swear I saw the visions of my great-aunts and my great-grandmother smiling at me all dressed in their beautiful gowns of the 1800s. In an instant, they vanished. 'Oh, my. This is strange.' Nevertheless, as I clutched my crystal horse, I wanted to believe, so I did.

I made my way back down the sixteen steps to the second floor of the house to my bedroom. I tried to compose myself as best I could before seeing my grandmother; to ask her about everything that had just happened. This was, of course, if she didn't ground me for the rest of my natural life.

Six
Octowallica Bim Bom

*I found Grandmother in the kitchen, snapping beans
as was her custom. She grew beans, okra, Brussels
sprouts, tomatoes and various herbs in a tidy garden
on the south side of the house. I do not ever recall my
grandmother buying vegetables at the market. She
said she enjoyed seeing things grow from seeds.*

*I pulled up a stool next to her and picked some
beans myself. I agonized over how to tell her about
my experience in the attic. She must have known I had
something to say, because not only was I holding onto
the crystal with one hand, I twirled my loose piece of
hair with the other. I figured the best way to say
something was to say it.*

*"Grandmother, I took the keys to the attic against
your rules. I had wanted something to do because I
was bored. You can punish me if you want. I
apologize, but I need to tell you about some very
strange things that happened to me up there and I
need some explanations."*

*Before letting her speak, I jumped right into my
experience. "I saw visions of my great-grandmother*

and two of her sisters in the most beautiful dresses I have ever seen. Then, a young girl all dressed in white appeared and spoke to me. She told me that I was the chosen one to solve a mystery and set her free. By the way, I was able to see through her. Who is she, and why was I able to see the three women? In addition, I also saw another young girl wearing a hat, who was sitting on one of the high rafters, and then later on, she cried. A black raven sat on the windowsill and pecked at the window. I saw him before on the day of the funeral. What am I supposed to do about all of this stuff?"

Grandmother had a curious expression on her face and looked like she wanted to interrupt me, but let me finish what I was saying before I could no longer speak.

I continued, "When you were a little girl living in this house, did you remember anything about a carousel located on the property? I thought I had been all over this estate and have never seen one. The girl said to find it. And, what was up with this black raven? Where did he come from?"

Then I asked, "How can I possibly solve some mystery I know nothing about – IN TWO WEEKS!"

I did not know what else to say at that point, and she took that opportunity to speak. I had been twisting my hair until it cut into my finger.

A half-smile crossed her face, and she wiped her

hands on her apron. After untwisting the hair from my finger, she looked upward, as if she were asking for guidance from above. Slowly, she turned to me, and in a stern voice said, "I am very disappointed that you went against my wishes and borrowed the keys to the attic. I will have to think of a punishment, but my reason for not wanting you to go up there was mainly that I did not want you to get hurt in case the floor gave way. I do forgive you. I once was a curious girl, too, and I knew one day you would want to explore the attic and would have all sorts of questions. I am surprised that one of the first things you mentioned is the carousel. I thought perhaps you would want to know about other things."

I wondered if she had also seen the visions of our ancestors. Was that what she meant by 'other things'? I wondered but kept quiet.

"The young girl you saw was Crystal Ann Le Grande, the only daughter of my great-grandfather's brother, Michael. They all lived together here on the estate. She was your namesake. Her mother, Emily, died when Crystal Ann was a baby, and the duties of rearing her fell to Michael. Usually men remarried quickly, just to have a woman to raise the children, but he loved his wife and couldn't love another, so he raised her alone. She was the apple of his eye, and he worshipped her. He wouldn't let his sister-in-law have anything to do with her care, and after a while, *she and my great-grandfather moved out of the house."*

Okay, so I was named for a distant cousin. How did she die? What's the mystery? Who was that other young girl; the one in the hat? All of these questions kept popping up. It was difficult to keep quiet, but out of respect for her, I did not say anything, as I was anxious for her to continue her story.

"Michael had bought the most beautiful white horse for Crystal Ann when she was eleven. His name was White Magic, and he could run like the wind and turned out to be a terrific jumper. He and Crystal Ann used to fly over the fences with ease. She was a great rider and won numerous ribbons in shows. To say that her father was proud would have been an understatement."

She continued, "Michael was a very talented wood-carver. He made our beautiful wooden staircase, the pieces over the doors in this house, and was commissioned by families to create statues of their horses as far away as Boston. He began carving wooden horses for Crystal Ann when she was just a baby. It was for a carousel he was building. He had an enclosure made for it on an adjoining piece of property. She was never allowed to go to that part of the estate."

I reasoned that must have been the building I had seen in the photo album, but kept quiet.

"Michael had just completed the last horse for the carousel. It was an exact replica of White Magic, complete with the beautiful tack that adorned the real horse. Crystal Ann and White Magic were out riding one afternoon and did not come back when she was supposed to. Calling to the caretakers on the estate, Michael and the other men took off to look for them. They found her lying on the ground. Obviously, she and White Magic had tried to jump a stone wall, and something happened that caused her to fall off. She had hit her head on the wall and had died instantly. The horse was so spooked; he took off into the deep forest at the back of the property, but eventually returned home."

Grandmother had stopped speaking as if trying to remember something more. This must have been very emotional for her. I do not think these things had been spoken about in generations.

"Octowallica bim bom," she uttered.

"Grandmother, what did you say?" The words were foreign to me. I sat very quiet.

As if in a trance, Grandmother swayed back and forth, and I was concerned that she might fall. As soon as I got near her, she snapped out of her trance and held out her hand to me. "Sit down, and I will tell you more of what I know."

Seven
The Horse in the Window

Not wanting to break whatever spell she had been under, I did as she requested. I wondered whether she was going to begin with 'Once upon a time' but decided not to ask her. What were those strange words she had uttered? What did they mean?

Grandmother began, "When I was a little girl living in this house, I sat at my grandmother's side as she worked on her needlepoint. She said it was important to make beautiful things that would tell a story about the family – things that would last a lifetime. The photos you have seen in the album upstairs are just a small part of the history of your family."

My grandmother spoke very slowly, as if to make sure I heard every word and visualize the story, just as she had done for all of my childhood years with her 'Once upon a time' stories.

"Michael had just finished carving the last horse, and after Crystal Ann died, he forbade anyone to go near the carousel. Nothing he could do could bring back his precious daughter. He threw himself into his

work, but his heart was not in it. He died shortly thereafter in a fire in the stable. The family is not completely sure as to how the fire started, but there was another person in there at the time, who also died."

"Because it was left abandoned for many years, an impenetrable thicket of vines and kudzu and weeds covered the carousel enclosure. I think somewhere there is a map of the adjoining property showing the location, but no one has ever tried to find it. They say that the area is haunted, and a ghost of a young girl lives out there in the woods. They call it Daphne's Forest."

"Who was she supposed to be?" I thought that was a reasonable question.

"I have no idea, except that that was not the first time the girl in a floppy hat had made an appearance. There was a lot of speculation as to who she was, and stories abounded within the family. We had no idea who she was, or why she was interested in our family. I understand that she has turned up from time to time."

Grandmother continued, "Many years after Crystal Ann and Michael died, my great-grandfather, whose name was Byron, moved back into the estate along with his wife and children. The house had been boarded up for over twenty years, and everything on the property was in pretty bad shape, especially the carousel. No one ever went near that location."

I could see this was difficult for her to relate, but I said nothing. I was more confused than ever. "Grandmother, what am I supposed to do to solve the mystery that Crystal Ann had mentioned? I don't even know where to begin."

Grandmother took the journals from me and began turning pages. She stopped at the old curling piece of paper on which was drawn unusual symbols and got that glazed look in her eyes again. She gently put down the journal and spoke.

"There might be a connection between the black raven you have seen, and the solving of the mystery. If the story is true, he had not always been a raven, but a young man who had worked as a groom on an estate in Atlanta. A spell was cast on him by an old woman, presumably a witch, and he had been turned into the raven. I recall his name was Cecil."

"Maybe he's one of the puzzle parts that will help you solve the mystery to release Crystal Ann, so she can cross over and be at peace. I believe that the strange words you heard me say are another part of the puzzle." Grandmother continued with her explanation. "I recall hearing about a series of three words or phrases, spoken by various members of the Le Grande family, but I only remember the one I spoke. I never put two and two together as them having anything to do with any kind of mystery. To me, *they were just funny sounding words that my mother said about some kind of puzzle pieces, a map, instructions, and a child's notebook. Maybe that is what she meant. I am sure there are other parts to the puzzle, though, like the symbols on the old piece of paper. I have always wondered about that, too. Then, there is the missing horse, White Magic, and the carousel."*

Oh, was that all? "Is this one of your stories?"

Grandmother said, "No I am completely serious." Handing me the keys, she suggested, "Take the journals back to the attic, or any place you'd like, and read everything and begin putting together the pieces of the puzzle. There isn't anything I can do to help you solve the mystery, since that responsibility has been given to you by Crystal Ann, but I'll be here for you if you need to ask any more questions."

Since it was getting late, and the rain was still coming down in buckets, I decided to put off reading through the journals until the next morning and put them back into the trunk in the attic. I did not see any of my ancestors lurking about and went downstairs and out onto the big swing on the veranda.

I needed some kind of direction, and spoke aloud to anyone who might listen, "Please show me where I am to begin to unravel this mystery." I closed my eyes, held onto my crystal, and heard the sound of calliope music in the distance, weaving its way through the wind, rain and trees. I felt strangely calm and soon fell asleep, curled up like a baby in the cushions of the swing.

Grandmother quietly opened the front door, walked onto the porch and covered me with a soft shawl. "You will find the answer, my darling."

I don't know how long I slept, but the rain had stopped, and looking up at the sky, a gazillion stars winked back at me. A big smile crossed my face, and I felt sure that the answers I needed would soon be revealed. I got up, went inside and headed up the main stairway, stopped on the landing that was eight steps from the bottom, and sat. The ceiling reached a height of over twenty feet at that point, and there was a beautiful stained-glass window about half way up. I had never really 'seen' it before, but the design was a carousel horse! This is a good sign, I thought. I continued on to the next eight steps to my bedroom on the second floor.

My bed looked very inviting to me, and before I knew it, I was asleep. Golden rings, a raven, horses, and images of my mother and father pointing to something, filled my dreams. I could not tell where I was supposed to look and kept turning around in circles until I was so dizzy, I fell down.

When I awoke the following morning, I lay on the floor, my comforter twisted around me. What had happened? I vaguely remembered the dream but couldn't make any sense out of it. All of the confidence I had the night before faded away, and I was more confused than ever.

"Okay, Crystal, what you need to do is wash your face, brush your teeth, pull your hair into a ponytail, and get dressed – but wait; I never undressed last night. I am still in my clothes. I really am losing it. Deep breaths, Crystal, you are going to need them." I ran from my bed and shed my clothes as I moved toward the bathroom and hit a cold shower.

Things like this just did not happen to anyone! Maybe to people in books or movies, but not to a girl from Georgia!

As I stood under the shower, I tried to form a plan. I would definitely eat something, go back to the attic, take one journal at a time and make notes. Perhaps that would lead me in the right direction. I felt better already. After drying off, and with a determined look on my face, I put on a clean pair of jeans and pulled my hair back into my usual ponytail. I quickly made my bed and put my dirty clothes away. Shoes or no shoes today? No shoes! So, barefoot and with great expectations, I slowly made my way down the eight stairs to the landing and looked up at the stained-glass window. It was not the design of the carousel horse I had seen the night before, but beautiful colorful flowers. Uh-oh! Did I dream that? Had it just been a sign? No time to answer those questions right then. I was on a mission. Look out; here I come!

Chloe stared at the three mannequins, "Okay, can you give me some answers to everything I just read?" They did not respond. Her grandma had been given a big problem to solve.

Because she was so involved, she had a hard time sleeping. Chloe could relate to that, especially right before a big test at school. Her grandma had a big test, too, only it involved a lot more than a good grade. Her grandma's Grandmother Bertie seemed like a really nice old granny, and Crystal seemed to be very happy as a young girl.

I wonder what happened to make Grandma such a sad old woman. The young girl had put a huge responsibility on her. Could that have been part of what made her sad? Chloe was so much a part of the story; once again, she mentally walked right into it.

Eight
The Mystery Begins

*I sang out a cheery, "Good morning, Grandmother,"
as I entered the kitchen. "Don't you think that it is just
the most beautiful day you have ever seen? The rain
always makes everything smell so good, and I am
ready to take on the mystery, so everything and
everyone can get back to normal."*

*Grandmother remarked, "You are certainly in a
good mood. I was not sure how you'd be feeling after
all of the information I filled your head with last
night. I knew it was not easy to digest everything, and
I have been giving things a lot of thought. If you want
to ignore it all and go back to what you were doing
before, I will certainly understand."*

*Knowing I was being tested, I said, "You and my
parents have always taught me to do what is right and
follow things through to the end. Daddy told me that
no unselfish act, done out of love for family, friend or
country will ever go unrewarded. I feel close to
Crystal Ann and Michael, and I cannot explain it. I
never knew either of them, but they were a part of the
family. This is all so unreal, and I know if I don't*

continue, I will never know the answers. I feel the right thing for me to do is to find out all I can about everything that had happened in the past, and if I am supposed to be the 'chosen' one, then how can I do anything but continue?"

Grandmother wiped her hands on her apron and came over to me. She held out her arms, and I fell into her warm body, just as I had done when I was a scared little girl. There is something about a grandmother's hug that makes everything all right.

"I am so proud of you, and I knew you would do the right thing. This will be the biggest adventure you have ever been on, and the excitement of that will make you press on to find a happy ending to this mystery. I will be anxious to learn what you uncover, but it is important for you to be careful, and take each step slowly. I know you are facing a deadline of two weeks but feel confident you will be successful."

"Gosh, I almost forgot about the deadline!" I thanked her with a kiss to her cheek and turned to run upstairs to the attic to continue my journey.

She stopped me. "Remember that your cousin Mathew is coming for a visit and is due today."

"Oh, piffle," using an expression I had heard her use. What was I going to do with him? Oh, well, I would deal with that when the time came.

I took the steps two at a time and when I reached the top, I cautiously entered the big room that was the attic. Everything seemed to be in order. No visions looked back at me, and the trunks were all in place where I had left them the night before. This time, when I opened the trunk lid, no glow appeared, and I raised the lid myself. I must say I was a little disappointed. Sitting in the top tray were the three journals and the photo album, just as before. I did not see any point in looking under the tray. I had more than I could handle right then. So, I decided that if I took one journal at a time, and read every page carefully, I could make notes of anything I thought might be important. There weren't any dates on any of the pages, and that meant I would have to figure out the sequence myself. I did the 'eeny-meeny-miney-moe' thing and picked up the chosen journal.

Back to my fluffy cushion, I sat down and carefully opened the journal. The beautiful handwriting was very much like what you would see in writings from the 1800s. The pages read like a diary, obviously written by Michael.

"Today our beautiful daughter, Crystal Ann, was born. She looks like an angel, just like her mother. We are so happy."

That was the first entry. It continued:

"I vow that I will do everything I can to make my daughter happy. She will have everything she wants, and I will spoil her. That is what I am supposed to do."

I found myself smiling, imagining how wonderful he must have felt, and knowing he had a beautiful daughter and wife. The next entry in the journal was about the sickness that Crystal Ann's mother had that eventually took her life. Tear stains on the ink helped me share his pain and grief as he wrote those lines.

As I turned the pages of the journal, Michael's writings became more and more scattered. He wrote of a mission he was on – to begin carving a carousel for his daughter. I remembered Grandmother telling me that Michael had carved the banisters and other wood pieces in this house. His work was incredible.

His beautiful child, now almost a year old, was showing a real love for ponies. She had walked very early and spent hours on her rocking horse. I stopped reading and thought what a coincidence it was that Crystal Ann had loved horses at such a tender age. I read on. Michael planned to make a small carousel for her, choosing replicas of six famous horses. He had a pavilion built to house the carousel, located on an adjacent piece of property, also owned by the Le Grande family. Michael had been very successful in his profession, and decided not to work any longer, carving for other people. He had enough money to last for years and vowed to give his daughter everything she would ever want.

Crystal Ann was just a baby when he began his special project. As she grew older, and the horses began to take shape, Michael seemed to be happier and calmer than he had ever been. Michael and Crystal Ann spent hours together every day, playing games, working puzzles, romping with their dogs – all of the things he knew his devoted wife would have done if she had lived. A nanny lived in the house, although he had rebelled against that – he wanted to take care of Crystal Ann all by himself. In addition, a caretaker and his family lived in a small house near where the carousel would be built. Finding the time to do his woodworking had to be done when he knew Crystal Ann was either napping or, once she was old enough, attending school.

I put the journal down and closed my eyes, imagining what their lives must have been like, living in this house (without running water, I might add), and trying to get through each day. Crystal Ann had just been a tiny baby when her mother died, so she didn't really know her, but Michael had been devoted to his wife, and she had loved him with all of her heart. I could relate to his pain, as I still missed my parents desperately.

The rest of the entries were about the wonderful things that Crystal Ann did in school. She was a good student and very popular with her friends. She used to write poems and short stories and won prizes for them. I wondered if he kept them, and where they might be.

Michael wrote in the journal from time to time, about the progress he made on the horses. He had completed three of them by the time Crystal Ann was six, and he reasoned that it took him about two years to carve and paint one horse, working a few hours a day when he could. The project would be completed in time for her twelfth birthday, as planned.

One particular entry caught my eye.

"Today is Crystal Ann's eleventh birthday. She is becoming such a lovely young lady. For a big surprise, I bought her the most magnificent white horse I could find. His name is White Magic, is well trained and has a pedigree as long as your arm. I know that doesn't mean anything to her, but I feel better, knowing he is well-bred."

I stopped reading, knowing what had happened later on, and silently wished I could have been able to warn her. Of course, that was impossible, but I had the thought anyway.

Michael's writing continued.

"Crystal Ann is so excited about the horse. I know she is a good rider, and feel comfort in knowing that the lessons have well prepared her to compete in the shows she has longed to participate in."

There were more entries, all about the horse shows, and the blue ribbons and trophies that Crystal Ann and White Magic had won. She was one happy girl, and Michael was elated. All of the carousel

71

horses had been finished and the final one was the most special of all. He carved a replica of White Magic that would take its place of honor on the carousel. He finished the final sanding and painting; his labor of love was complete.

A very short sentence followed but did not appear to have been written by Michael. I think it was his brother, my great-great-grandfather, Byron, who wrote:

"Today our precious Crystal Ann was killed trying to jump a wall with White Magic. Michael is devastated, and I don't think he will ever get over it. The horse had run off but came back a few days later. Michael is trying so hard to deal with what happened and has thrown himself into his work."

I turned the pages, looking for more entries, but there was only one, written a few weeks after the accident that took Crystal Ann's life. My great-grandmother, Eufaula, wrote,

"Michael died today. He had gone to the stables to see White Magic. Something caused a fire, and he died trying to save a young friend of Crystal Ann's. We will board up the house and maybe one day there will once again be laughter here, but not now, not soon."

There were no more entries in Michael's journal.

Chloe awoke from her trip into yesterday, sat back,

gently put the journal down in her lap, and remained quiet. She audibly sniffed and realized that she had been crying.

Why didn't Grandma ever tell me about any of that? She must have been totally crushed with all of that responsibility put on her shoulders. How could she stand it? Was she able to do what she was supposed to do?

She set the journal back on top of the trunk and headed to find Grandma and ask for the rest of the story. The door was closed, and when she tried to open it, it didn't budge. She was locked in. *OMG, this can't be happening.* She yelled at the top of her lungs, "Grandma, help me, I'm locked in the attic, and the key is on the outside. Help me." The only thing she heard was the distant thunder. That's why she hadn't heard the door when it slammed shut, and probably why her grandma hadn't heard her cry for help. A new scent of gardenias again filled the air beside her. She sensed someone else besides the mannequins was there with her. "Who are you? Please help me get out of here!" Nothing.

Chloe didn't know if there was a light up there, and she had a great fear of the dark. She turned around and located a switch near the door. She snapped the switch, and the room partially filled with a dim light from the single bulb that hung from the ceiling. Very slowly, she headed back to the trunk

73

and once again sat down on the floor and resumed reading this incredible story. It was a difficult task, reading in the low light, but Chloe did not want to stop. She was once again swept away with the story.

Nine
Sherlock Holmes Shows Up

I reviewed in my mind all of the happenings of the past couple of days and was not any closer to figuring things out than I was when I began. What did I know? My great-great uncle, Michael, was a famous wood carver. He carved beautiful wood pieces in my grandmother's house. His wife had died shortly after giving birth to their daughter, Crystal Ann. As a devoted father, he wanted to do everything he could to make her happy.

I had had a visit from Crystal Ann – or actually her ghost, asking me to solve a mystery so she and her father could be reunited, and she could pass over to the other side. That left me clueless! A young girl in a hat, carrying a gardenia, had appeared for some reason. I did not know who she was. A black raven, like the one I saw the day of my parents' funeral, begged for my attention in the attic; I found a photo album filled with pictures of my ancestors. Three journals contained Michael's writings. Tucked into the back of one of the journals was a folded piece of paper, with strange words and symbols on it. All I could think was, "HELP!"

I must have uttered those words aloud, because about that time, I heard the sound of footsteps coming up the sixteen steps. Uh-oh. I turned around, and there stood my seven-year-old cousin, Mathew. I had forgotten all about him. What am I going to do now? He's going to get in the way. And then he'll think I am crazy. I was not so sure I wasn't.

"Hi," I said to Mathew, trying to sound grown up. "What's new?" What a dumb question that was. Come on, Crystal, calm down.

Mathew answered with his usual, "Hiya, cuz, what are you doing? Can I help?"

I had to think fast. I could not let him know everything that had happened, but I had to continue to search for answers. What could I say to him to let him think we would be doing something together, and not reveal the honest to goodness thing I was doing?

"Hey, Matt, I was just looking through all of these old trunks. There are some neat things in there – old pictures, old clothes, and some trinkets that used to belong to my ancestors. It's like looking through history books." I knew how much Matt hated history, and thought if I emphasized the word history, he would not want to become involved. I was very wrong.

Matt exclaimed, "How neat is that! I think if we find out things about what went before, we can improve on what came after. My history teacher last year, Miss Jergens, really impressed me with that."

76

So, my little cousin, Matt, had such a crush on his history teacher, that he really wanted to learn. Great! Why couldn't he just have stayed the obnoxious little brat he had always been? Playing along with him, I said, "I think that is great. Are you saying that you would like to spend hours with me, going through every piece of paper, every hat, dress, necklace, book, and search under things, to find out what it is I am researching?"

Matt looked at me like he was going to back away, but instead, he asked, "Where do I start? This could be fun. I might even become the next Sherlock Holmes!"

I was doomed!

"Okay, Matt, here's the story. I am trying to figure out a puzzle, and I have less than two weeks to do it. I am looking for anything with strange words written on it. I don't know what they all mean, but I do know there is an old piece of paper that has some strange symbols and words. I need the instructions on how to make everything go together, so I—" I paused because Matt was standing there with his mouth open, his eyes wide, and looked like he was going to either laugh or cry. "What's wrong?" I asked.

"Are you making up a story like Aunt Bertie used to tell you, or has your imagination gone crazy? You aren't making any sense. It sounds like something out of a bad dream. Fill me in on the details, and then maybe I'll know what in the world you are talking *about and whether I want to help."*

I pointed to a spot in front of the trunk with the top open and told him to sit down, and I would tell him everything that had happened. "But you have to promise not to interrupt me, or laugh, or roll your eyes."

He grinned. "Go on." He sat down as I instructed and made a zip sign across his lips. Very funny, I thought, as I proceeded to fill him in on everything I knew; everything that had happened from the first visit to the attic.

When I had finished, Matt sat very quietly, and no, he didn't roll his eyes, and didn't interrupt, but he did look like he was going to run!

He stood and came over to me, lifted my head up with his fingers under my chin, and said, "That was the most unbelievable, wonderful story I have ever heard. Do you think I'll be able to see the ghost or the raven, and what do you think it all means? Why do you think you were picked to solve it, and what do you want me to do?" Jumping up and down, he remarked that this was going to be the most fun he had had in a long time and could not wait to get started.

I was not prepared for his reaction. I was waiting for the rolling eyes thing. This time, I was the one rolling my eyes with a big grin on my face. "Okay, Sherlock. You and I are a team."

Ten
More Weird Words

While Mathew and I were in the attic, reviewing all that had happened and the things that needed to be done in order to find the answer, Grandmother was in her bedroom resting. The past couple of days had been very tiring, and because she wasn't a young woman anymore, she was entitled to rest. Actually, she took a nap every afternoon. She said it was very refreshing.

Matt removed the top tray, and pulled one of several folders, each one labeled as 'Incantation.' He turned to me and asked, "What does this word mean?"

"They are the use of spells or charms spoken or sung as part of a ritual of magic."

"What are they used for?"

"They are used to make things happen." Trying to make a comparison, I said, "It is like when magicians say, 'abracadabra' when they make a rabbit appear out of a hat. The words are an incantation. Why did you ask?"

"I just found a box full of them."

I walked over to the trunk where Matt held an armful of folders. There must have been twenty of them. Wait a minute! They must have belonged to Michael and his family. Why were they kept in a box and not just written down in the journals?

I decided to forge ahead and open the first folder. About the same size as a piece of notebook paper, it had been sealed with wax. I had seen a package like that in a stationery store once, along with a metal 'seal' that pressed the hot wax in order to seal two pieces of paper together, and usually had the initials or crest of the person using it. The folder read MLG, I assumed, for Michael Le Grande.

"Matt, we'll wait until Grandmother is awake before we open the folder. With the way things are going, there's no telling what might happen. I've received all of the surprises I need, and don't think I can handle any more ghosts or whatever else might appear."

"I want to open the folders now."

At seven, what could you expect? Since I was almost grown, I tried to understand. Secretly, I was curious about the contents of the box, but decided not to let him know that. Instead, I suggested, "Let's look in the other trunks, to see what's in them." He was all for that idea.

Once again, when I approached the second trunk, the lid flew open, and then closed again. Matt

80

jumped back so quickly, he fell on the floor and screamed, "Crystal!" I couldn't help but laugh, remembering the way I had felt when I visited the attic for the first time. I did feel bad for the little guy, though.

He rushed to me and wrapped his arms around my waist. "What's happening?"

This was my brave, smart-aleck cousin, melting like a cube of ice on a hot stove. I held him, "It's okay. I've already had that experience, and it was totally harmless. They just want us to look in that trunk."

"Who are they, and why haven't you told me about trunks that move?"

"I assure you it's all right." However, I left out some of the details about my first encounter in the attic. "It seems that the visions I had seen know something we don't and are trying to help us find the answers. What we need to do is look in the trunk. Are you okay with that?"

In his very brave voice he assured me, "I'm fine now, and what's a little ghost anyway. Go ahead, open it up!"

Matt was clearly shaken, but I walked over to the trunk. When I did, the lid opened up all by itself. Again, I thought Matt was going to break and run, but he stood his ground and looked at me with his eyes wide open. I peered inside. No ghosts, no glow, just one crumpled piece of paper sitting all by itself in the top tray. I looked at Matt, who was visibly disappointed, and turned away, muttering to himself. He sat on the cushion and stared at something at the window.

I reached for the paper, wondering what was coming next. As I straightened the piece of paper, I felt someone else watching me. And the scent of gardenias filled the air. Matt and I were alone, and I didn't see Crystal Ann this time.

Parts of words and something about a map that would lead us to the carousel filled the paper. Crystal Ann had told me to find it. What was the importance of the carousel in reuniting Crystal Ann and Michael? I had remembered the strange words that Grandmother had uttered, 'Octowallica bim bom.' A different set of words on the page jumped out at me and caused my heart to pound harder. 'Doo doffa dinglediffer.'

Wanting to include Matt, who had been sitting on the cushion, I suggested, "Let's lift out the tray and look in the bottom of the trunk." I turned toward where he had been sitting, but my brave detective seemed to have disappeared. Maybe he needed to get a drink of something, or maybe he was hungry. Most kids his age were always hungry!

I lifted the tray and set it on the floor. Inside, piles of what appeared to be tablecloths, napkins, samplers, and other beautiful linens verified

82

Grandmother's story about the needlepoint her grandmother used to stitch. I had never done any of that kind of stitching but could see the results of loving hands that had worked on those pieces. There were embroidered edges on napkins and hankies, crocheted doilies, needlepoint samplers with different writings and pictures and words like, 'Bless This Home'. How wonderful they were! We don't do that kind of things nowadays, do we? I seem to remember seeing my grandmother knit and crochet, but nothing like that!

I sat on my knees in front of the trunk, and almost fell over backwards when the raven pecked at the partially open window again. He startled me, and I asked, "What do you want?" He kept pecking, but I didn't want to open the window all the way and let him in. I didn't think he would hurt me, but he continued to get my attention. I was holding a folded piece of needlepoint. I heard the raven again and looked at him. He nodded up and down. "Do you mean the answer to my search is stitched on this sampler?" I gently unfolded the linen.

The stitching was of a house with trees, flowers, and the hitching post; similar to the house I was living in and filled much of the picture. A carousel appeared in the background. Under the picture were these words: 'The old and the new will unite when words and deeds are joined together. 'Hipta-minica-

wonga-songa-bomptalaria'.

Oh, my, more of those weird words. Okay, now I had three sets of words. They might be instructions of some kind. I looked at the window, but the raven had flown away. I decided I would take this sampler, along with the sealed folder and the old paper, downstairs to Grandmother. I didn't want to wake her, so I would wait awhile before returning downstairs.

Speaking to no one, I asked, "How do the series of words connect with Crystal Ann and Michael, the carousel, White Magic and the raven? He seemed more like a human than a bird."

Wait! Grandmother told me that a young stable boy named Cecil had been turned into a black raven. Was that him? Yeah right, this was the 1950's and things like that only happened in Walt Disney movies, like when the Fairy Godmother was able to turn six white mice into six white horses in Cinderella. Oh, I was all right, standing there talking to myself! Time was not on my side, and I was beginning to get nervous. Where did Matt go? I knew he was going to be a problem. This was not the best time for him to come for a visit.

I refolded all of the heirlooms and gently put them back into the bottom of the trunk; all but the needlepoint sampler, still sensing another presence.

Armed with my treasures, I took one more look around and headed back downstairs.

Eleven
The Old Will Unite with the New

I almost tripped going down the stairs, and juggled my treasures when I bumped into Matt, who charged up the stairs, out of breath.

"I've been exploring, and I think I found the carousel. I had been watching the raven on the window sill and wanted to see if I could catch him. By the time I got outside, he flew away. So, I followed him."

"Calm down, Matt. Tell me why you think you have found the carousel. The carousel isn't even on this piece of property."

"I knew you were busy looking in the trunks, and it felt really creepy up there, with all of the strange things that had happened. Besides, I figured that I should spend more time outside."

That made sense for a seven-year-old.

"Matt, we'll have to wait until tomorrow when it's daylight. By the time we get to the carousel, if you really did find it, it'll be dark. I sure don't want to go out there at night."

"You're a chicken; not a detective, and after

wanting me to help you don't want to see what I had found." Matt hung his head low and pouted.

"It wouldn't be sensible for us to go to the other piece of property this late in the evening, especially with all of the things that have been going on. How do we know all of the visions are friendly? Maybe there are bad spirits out there. They love the dark and probably aren't around in the daytime. Wouldn't it make more sense to search in the daytime? To tell you the truth, I'm wiped out. I am really happy that you think you found the carousel, and maybe that will help fill in the holes in my puzzle. We'll start very early in the morning." I looked at Matt, to see if he would agree to my plan.

He said, "It sounds like a good deal. When are we going to eat?" And off he ran.

I entered the kitchen to find Grandmother standing in front of the stove, stirring something that smelled wonderful. She wanted to know if we had been having a good time. She had napped a little longer than she had wanted, but dinner would be ready in just a few minutes. Homemade chili, hot dogs, and root beer floats. Grandmother made the best chili I had ever tasted, and I loved hot dogs. I couldn't remember the last time we had that kind of dinner. It must have been because Matt was here.

"Matt found over twenty folders marked 'incantations', and we brought the one that was sealed

with the MLG seal. I figured it was Michael's because of the initials. I also found a piece of linen in the bottom of the second trunk, with a needlepoint picture and some new words I have not heard before. Is this part of the mystery?"

Matt rushed into the kitchen and added, "And I followed the raven down to the back part of the property. I think I found where the carousel is."

Grandmother's face lit up with her million-dollar smile, as she sat down on a stool nearby. "You are really a good team. I'm sure that Crystal Ann made the right decision when she chose you to help her. After dinner, we'll look at everything you found so far and try to decipher what it all means."

We pigged out on hot dogs and chili, and I had two root beer floats. When we couldn't eat another bite, Grandmother suggested we go into the front parlor and spread our treasures out on the coffee table.

"Let's see what you have here," Grandmother said. "These old drawings and symbols are very primitive, like things on a treasure map. I believe the words I had spoken, which came to me after you told me of your experience in the attic, may be the first series of words you will need to combine with the others. I haven't spoken or thought of those words in over sixty years. I remember hearing them as a young child and didn't even know what they were until a couple of days ago. The second set of words written on the single sheet of crumpled paper that Matt found may, or may not be actually in second position, but is very much a part of the puzzle."

Matt and I sat very still while Grandmother spoke. My heart pounded so hard, I was sure they could hear it. Were we close to solving this mystery? I had used up two days already and still had to decipher the code of the symbols, find the carousel and White Magic, and bring it all together.

"Grandmother, what does the message on the sampler mean? Are the words stitched on it the final group to put with the others? I just don't understand what the message means about old and new mixing together with words and deeds, or whatever it said. I am hoping you have an idea."

She sat back in the cushions of the antique sofa and thoughtfully replied, "It must mean that the old – or the life of Crystal Ann, her mother and father and White Magic, plus the new – you, Matt and me working together, along with the 'deeds', that is, the research we are doing in love, are the key to finding the answer to the puzzle. I think there must be something else in the 'deeds' category because we haven't figured out where the carousel and the raven fit. And no one seems to know where White Magic is. I don't think your sleuthing is finished yet."

Matt asked, "What is sleuthing?"

88

I told him, "It means detective work, Sherlock. We'll plan to get right on it early in the morning." I hoped that the answer would satisfy my little cousin. "I'm off to bed. See you in the morning."

Matt plopped down on an ottoman and said, "I'm not ready to leave yet. What about the sealed folder? Should we open it?"

Grandmother said, "I think we need to wait until everything is in place."

Since I trusted her, I told her I agreed and looked over at Matt, who nodded his head, 'yes'.

She gave me a big hug. "I am very proud of you. It is a wonderful thing you are doing. Remember, we are all supposed to do things for others, and even though this is a tough job, with your wonderful helper, pardon me, I mean assistant, and I have every confidence that you will figure it out in no time." Then she added her terrific smile to the mix!

We thanked her, and although my head was full of questions, I went along with the program hoping the answers would drop in my lap. I said goodnight and called Matt, 'Sherlock'. He laughed and threw a sofa pillow at me.

I ran up the stairs, two at a time, and stopped to catch my breath on the landing. Flowers still appeared in the stained-glass window, so I guessed the spirits had gone to bed, too.

Chloe stopped reading and stood to stretch her stiff legs. The dim light had begun to hurt her eyes. She had lost track of time, and the cell phone battery had run down. There she was, stuck in the attic and her stomach growled. Even chicken cordon bleu would taste good to her now. Her grandma couldn't hear her, and Chloe believed that if she knew she was in the attic, she might leave her up there to teach her a lesson. What if Grandma got sick and needed her, or an ambulance, or something like that? Who would be there to help her? These were all new feelings for Chloe, and she realized she was envious of Crystal's relationship with her grandmother. They trusted and had respect for one another. What a wonderful thing to have someone care that much about you. She recognized that she wanted to have a relationship with her grandma, and really needed it.

To stop herself from the 'what if's' and other questions, she sat back down on the floor and returned to the past.

Twelve
Matt Meets a Stranger

I woke up at five-thirty the next morning and lay there trying to decide what to do first. I knew Matt wanted to head out in the direction of where he saw the carousel. I wanted to find it, too, but for some reason, I was hesitant. I held on to my crystal horse and silently asked for confidence. The crystal started warming up, and soon I was all right again. In a minute, there was a knock on my door. "Come on in, Matt."

"You said we were going to start early, and I haven't slept a wink."

Was this the little pest that used to drive me nuts? No, this was a committed detective, geared up for the adventure of his life, and he didn't want to miss any of it. I secretly was glad he was there. I needed all of the help I could get.

"Okay, Sherlock," I said. "Give me fifteen minutes, and I'll meet you in the kitchen. I need to shower and dig out a pair of old shoes. If we are going to tramp around on the property, our feet should be protected. What are you wearing?"

He stuck one foot up. "They are my lucky old tennis shoes, and they never let me down."

"Right!"

"I'm hungry, too. I'll go check to see if Aunt Bertie is up."

"Don't wake her. We can get our own breakfast and pack a lunch. It's too early to bother her, and this is something we should do ourselves. If we need her help, we can come back to the house. Now, get out so I can get ready!"

Standing under the warm water, I heard the calliope music. I vowed that this was going to be the day I found out where that was coming from.

The passage written in the journal by my great-great-grandmother, Eufaula, indicated that the carousel pavilion had long since been abandoned. The building would obviously be overgrown with weeds. It would take a lot of cutting and digging to uncover it. I'm just a girl, a tomboy, but still a girl. Matt is only seven and not that strong. We would have to stop at the tool shed and gather up some tools to help us.

I was still standing in the shower when I heard a knock on the door. "Crystal, are you still in there? I want to get going," Matt called out.

"I'll be out in a sec," I answered. "Go back downstairs." I turned off the water and grabbed a towel from a hook on the wall. As I dried off, I couldn't help but think about young Crystal Ann, and what she had to go through without running water. That must have been very hard. I was glad I lived in this century!

I quickly dressed, tied my hair back in a ponytail, and grabbed my old tennis shoes, a pair of socks and started for the door. Oops, I had forgotten to make my bed. Grandmother would not have liked that a bit. I made the bed, making sure it didn't have any wrinkles, and took one last look around the room. Sitting there on my dresser was my prized possession, my crystal horse necklace that now had the golden ring on it. I could not make it through the day without that treasure. I removed the golden ring and put it in my jewelry box, fastened the special clasp on the gold chain and ran out the door.

As I walked down the stairs, I felt a presence watching me. I glanced up at the stained-glass window, and there it was again; a beautiful white carousel horse. In a corner of the landing, the vision of a man pleaded with me with outstretched arms. He held his hands to his heart and motioned above in a prayerful manner. He was dressed like some of the pictures in the photo albums. "Are you Michael?" The man nodded, 'yes', and then faded away. Oh, boy, I knew I was either going crazy or would wake up and find that this had all been a dream! Or, maybe that was a good sign. Michael looked very sad, and the weight of my task was heavier than it had ever been before. I must not fail.

I continued down the stairs and headed for the kitchen. Matt and Grandmother stood at the sink. "Good morning, Grandmother, I hope we didn't wake you. We were going to eat something and make a lunch and then be on our way out to search for the carousel."

She turned and said, "Good morning to you, too, Miss Crystal. Look at you in shoes, no less." She broke into her big grin and gave me a warm hug.

I needed that. She definitely had a knack for making you feel good and happy at the same time.

"Matt told me you both have been up for a long time. I knew you were anxious to get going, and as soon as your helper finishes taking the tops off of the strawberries, you can have bacon and strawberry pancakes."

"Yum! I love your strawberry pancakes." She topped them off with fresh whipped cream and shook a little powdered sugar over the top. "Maybe I'll just stay here and eat pancakes all day!" I laughed at myself thinking that.

"I made lunches for you two in case you lose track of time."

"Grandmother, you're the best."

I told her and Matt about seeing Michael and how sad he looked. If someone had told me that I

would be having conversations with ghosts, or
spirits, or whatever they were, I would have said they
were crazy. I felt as though my heart would break if I
didn't help Crystal Ann and Michael.

Chloe's stomach growled, and she realized how
hungry she was. The light grew dimmer, and she
began to think of the possibility of being in the dark
alone. "Okay, girl, think." She remembered seeing a
tin box on top of a shelf that contained candles and
matches. Standing, she walked over to the shelf, and
when she removed the top, she sagged with relief to
find two white candles and a small box of matches.
The light was still bright enough to read for a while,
and she didn't want to use up the candles until she
really needed them. She returned to her reading.

My grandmother is the best! We pigged out on
pancakes until we could hardly move. It was with a
great deal of effort that Matt and I slid off the stools
and slowly made our way to the back door. I turned
to look at my young cousin, and he was not moving
as fast as he usually did. I had to laugh, because we
both felt like we were big round doughboys instead of
healthy young children. I vowed at that moment,
never to stuff myself again!

"Come on, slowpoke," I called out to Matt, as I
headed out the door. "We have a lot to do today."

Saying goodbye to Grandmother, we promised to be back before it got dark. She blew both of us kisses and turned back to the sink, a big smile on her face.

Matt followed me out the door, carrying our lunch, which I had left on the counter. My mind was on things other than food at that point. We didn't say much as we walked toward the back of the property, past the carriage house (now the garage), and then I remembered that I had wanted to stop at the tool shed. The shed was about ten feet square, with a small door and two small windows. I never understood why they would put windows in a tool shed, but I'm sure whoever built it had a good reason.

Matt asked, "Are we really going to go in there? It doesn't look so good from where I am standing. Maybe there are rats and spiders and old ghosts living here." Scrunching up his face, he said, in no uncertain terms, "I hate spiders! You go first, and I'll keep watch."

This was my brave wannabe Sherlock Holmes, and he was chickening out on me. I wished he hadn't said anything about rats and spiders. I didn't mind the ghosts, but I, too, didn't like rats and spiders. I couldn't back down now. I needed some kind of tool to carry with us, even if it was just to bang around in the weeds to scare off critters. And snakes! I had forgotten about snakes. This was summertime, after all, and I had read that snakes would come out to sun themselves when the weather was warm. Was the end result of all of our adventures going to be worth everything we were going through? Yes! I talked myself into it. Cautiously, I opened the door; or rather tried to open the door. I didn't know when it had been opened last, but it wasn't cooperating now.

"Matt, you're going to have to help me. I can't get the door open. Matt?" Where did he go? I thought he might have decided to leave me behind to search on his own. You don't know about seven-year-olds.

I just had that thought, when he came running back from around the far side of the shed, and called out, breathlessly, "There is an old man sitting on a wooden barrel out back. He smiled at me but didn't say anything. He scared me."

"Calm down and show me what you saw. We don't have anyone else living here. There is just Grandmother and me, and now you, visiting us. Are you sure you saw someone? I bet because you ate so much, it has affected your brain."

"Very funny," Matt answered. "I know I saw an old man back there. At first, I thought he might have been one of Michael's carvings that you had told me about, but he waved and smiled at me. Come on, I'll show you."

I followed Matt to the back of the shed, but no one was there, so I returned to the front door. It was time for me to roll my eyes, but somehow, looking at *the expression on Matt's face, I decided I wouldn't do that. Poor kid, this must have been a lot for him to swallow. Boy, he'd have some stories to tell his friends when he went back to San Francisco.*

"We need to see if we can get the door open. One, two, three," I puffed, as we tried to get the old door open. "Again, one, two, three." The door did not cooperate. It was stuck solid. "Maybe I can crawl through one of the windows, if I can get it open, and hand you the tools."

That sounded like a good idea, but when I suggested that because he was smaller than I was, he should be the one to crawl through the window, he stomped his foot, and said, "NO!"

"Some brave assistant you are!" Okay, so I tried all of the windows, and none of them wanted to open, either. Just one last time, I tried the door, and with one gentle tug, it opened. The windows allowed just enough morning light in to let us see well enough.

I cautiously stepped inside, and what caught my eye was an amazing array of all kinds of tools; shovels and rakes, an ax, various mallets and a wheelbarrow. On a high table, I think it was called a workbench, was a big assortment of knives that I guessed were the tools my great-great uncle had used to carve the beautiful horses and other pieces so many years ago. There weren't any modern things there, but everything that was there was in perfect condition. I almost didn't want to touch anything. I walked away from the workbench and picked up a shovel and a rake that were hanging on wall hooks. They would have to do for the time being. Turning toward the door, I said, "We should go find that carousel." But Matt was not there. Now where had he gone?

Thirteen
The Old Man

I turned to close the door to the tool shed and bumped into the old man that Matt had been telling me about. I almost fell down, not only from shock, but because I almost lost my balance. I pulled myself up to my full height and tried to sound very grown up as I inquired, "Who are you, and what may I do for you?" Of course, my knees were shaking so hard I felt I might fall down. I clutched the pendant.

The old man smiled broadly and said, "My name is Jonas. I was one of the caretakers on this estate a long time ago and have been sent to help you with your quest, Miss Crystal." He bowed like a gentleman and removed his cap.

This was amazing! I was living in the twentieth century, having a conversation with a man who, if what he said was true, had lived in the nineteenth century.

I cleared my throat. "I am very pleased to meet you, Jonas. How did you know my name?"

"A big bird told me. I knew Crystal Ann and her father very well. My father before me had been in

charge of taking care of the grounds and the calliope on the carousel."

Pinch me, I am dreaming! I said, "It's impossible! There is no way you and I can be having this conversation. You are way over a hundred years old, I am almost twelve, and none of this makes any sense. I can see you as easily as I can see the rake in my hand, and yet it shouldn't be happening at all. I saw a vision of Crystal Ann in the attic and three of my other ancestors, but I could see through them. They were like ghosts, and you are like a real human being! Can you please explain that?"

Jonas sat on the old barrel where Matt had first seen him; scratched his chin and slowly told me the following story:

"My family had been slaves on this estate but were treated more like family. I grew up not realizing that we were different. We were caretakers and groomsmen and maids. It surprised me that after I died, I was still here on the estate, but since I was happy in my work and on this land, maybe it was heaven. My heaven. I look real to you because it is real to me. I am able to materialize when needed. It is not time for me to leave, so I stick around with occasional appearances. There is simply a lot of unfinished business here."

Pinch me again! If this all hadn't been so exciting, I would have thought we all were nuts. "I remember hearing that there had been a caretaker who worked for Michael who had been with him when Crystal Ann was found. You must also have been grieving for her after all this time, and if I can solve the mystery I have been asked to do, then you too will finally be able to rest." A deep sense of excitement rushed over me.

Jonas nodded and continued, "I had been content where I was, until a certain lovely little lady found me and asked me to help you get on the right track to finding the answers to the puzzle, so she can be at peace."

"Would her name happen to be Crystal Ann?"

"Of course," Jonas said. "She was such a lovely child. Her father loved her more than life itself, and it had hurt me deeply after she died. She would have loved the carousel and especially the beautiful carved model of White Magic. It would have been the happiest day of her life, if—" and Jonas couldn't finish his story, except to say, "I assume that you know what happened."

I turned to him and said, "Yes, I know the story. I know how sad everyone was when she died. She came to me for only a minute in the attic. She was so pretty and seemed desperate, as she said, to cross over. I want more than anything to help her. She told me to find the carousel. This morning, Michael visualized and pleaded with me to find the answers to *the puzzle. Maybe I can put the rest of the pieces together, but I don't know exactly how to do that."*

Jonas stood held out his hand. "Follow me, and we will do that together. I feel you are a lot like Crystal Ann."

I was flattered, of course, but what would Grandmother think about my meeting with Jonas? However, he was a ghost, and therefore in my mind, was totally harmless. As we walked along, I turned to Jonas and asked, "Did you happen to see where my cousin; the little boy you saw earlier, disappeared to? I can't keep track of him. And, by the way, how did the door open so easily, when it was impossible to open it before? Did you do it?"

"Guilty as charged about the door, and I don't know where your cousin is at the moment, but I'm sure he will turn up soon. He's probably a pretty smart boy doing some curious exploring somewhere. As far as the issue of the door, I think we may have another presence to deal with; a young girl about your age. Crystal Ann had a friend from school who used to come to the estate a lot. She was an orphan, I think. Many stories have been told about what happened to her. The truth is that she died in the fire at the stables. Her spirit is said to live in the forest on the next property. People are afraid to go near that place. They call it Daphne's Forest."

"Grandmother mentioned that to me. Why would

she want to keep us from completing our mission? Jonas, there is also a black raven here that keeps appearing in my life." I chattered on and then took a deep breath when a smile appeared on his face.

Matt ran up to us panting and grabbed me around the waist. "I saw a ghost – a young girl wearing a big hat carrying a gardenia. She scared me, and I couldn't move!" Pointing to Jonas, Matt said, "See, I told you I saw an old man. Do you know the girl ghost, too?" He looked scared, and said, "I think I'm going to go home."

I had never seen Matt like that. He was always kind of a smart-aleck, and a pain to be around, but my heart ached to see him frightened. "You were just startled. That's why you couldn't move." I took his hand, and we sat on an old fallen log. I gently told him, "Matt, this is Jonas. He was the caretaker on the estate when Crystal Ann lived here and is going to help us. He unlocked the shed door and can be trusted. He said the girl usually hangs out on the next property in the forest. She, for some reason, has materialized, sort of."

Matt asked, "Maybe she doesn't want us to solve this mystery. Can't we just tell her we would like to be her friend? Then maybe she'd go away."

Leave it to an innocent child to come up with that kind of logic. "We won't let her get the best of us, and Jonas said she won't hurt us, but maybe she doesn't want us to succeed in finding the carousel. She just wants to be the center of attention." I added, "Matt, are you in or out?"

Looking relieved, Matt heaved a big sigh. "I just had a temporary meltdown. I'll be fine." He extended his hand to Jonas, "It is nice to meet you, and I wonder, by the way, whether that girl has a name. Just in case I run into her again, I want to be polite." He smiled his semi-famous grin and looked down at the ground and kicked at the dirt with his shoe.

Jonas answered, "I think her name may be Daphne."

Matt was still a little shaken. "That wasn't a nice thing for her to do, you know, scaring me like that. Boy, wait until I see her again, I'll—"

I interrupted Matt's tirade. "Now, stop it. You can't fight with a ghost. You will never win. Besides, she is just a girl! We need to get on to what we are supposed to be doing. Time's a-wastin', as they say."

Fourteen
Following the Raven

As we walked along the path leading to the back part of the property, Jonas told us about his life at Le Grande Manor. He had just been a young boy when he and his parents were slaves at the Le Grande estate, and his father was an extremely hard worker. He found himself doing more than just taking care of the grounds. When Michael began work on the carousel, Jonas' father built the calliope. "He was an extremely talented musician, and this was a dream job for him." Tears formed in Jonas' eyes as he spoke.

I smiled. "I think it is very important that we find the carousel, because one of the pieces of the puzzle seems to be about the carousel and the music. I have heard the calliope music a lot ever since I was a little girl. Now I think that it is more important than I had first believed."

Changing the subject, he related, "Michael and Crystal Ann would take long rides in an old buggy that had been in the family for years. There was a small, strong pony that they hitched to and rode all over the estate. Crystal Ann had only been three at the time and squealed with delight when her daddy let her take the reins. Of course, the little pony was well trained and didn't need to have anyone in control, but Michael didn't tell her that. He told her what a big girl she was, and that someday she would have her own big horse to ride. She loved that idea."

"It must have been a wonderful time for both of them," I replied. "I can remember doing things with my dad, and they are very special memories."

Jonas said, "They were always very close, and had it not been for the loss of Crystal Ann's mother, their life would have been perfect."

"That's why I believe it's so important for all of us to figure out how to get them back together forever."

Matt had been trailing along pretty closely behind us, and suddenly he screamed, "Leave me alone!" The raven was pecking at his hat and vigorously flapping his wings. Matt ran to me, and the next thing we saw, the raven had a snake in his beak and flew off with it.

"Wow, did you see him? He saved me from getting bitten by that snake." Huffing and puffing, Matt was pulling on his hair, slapping his pant leg with his hat, and jumping from foot to foot. "That was pretty neat, huh?"

"Yes, it was pretty neat. The raven is like your guardian angel looking out for you, and that is pretty special. "

Jonas remarked, "We should make a plan. You have less than a week until your deadline. If we don't rush into things, we can find everything you need, and still have time left over. It is important to stick closely together and watch where we walk, since most of the paths have been washed away by the storm. I know there is a map of the adjoining property somewhere. Look around for it or ask your grandmother where it might be. Michael had one made before building the pavilion. If you still hear the calliope, then it must still be in operation. We should listen for the music to lead us to the carousel. "

"What do you mean; the calliope must still be in operation? You're kidding, right? Oh, right, this is all just a dream, and the ghosts are playing tricks and taking rides on a carousel with music playing. But I do hear the music, so it must be true, right?"

Jonas had to laugh at me because I guess I looked really weird and was talking in circles. "Don't dismiss something just because you can't see it, Crystal. Do you agree?"

"Yes. Everything is just so strange, and it takes a little getting used to. I believe we are headed in the right direction, but the property is so huge, we shouldn't go too far in any one day, because we still have to go back to the house. And that will take time. Grandmother mentioned that there is a map of the *property. I'll ask her if she knows where it might be when we get back to the house."*

I thought that was a pretty good statement, but when I looked at Matt, he cocked his head, and sarcastically said, "And they say blondes are dumb." Off he ran laughing, and the raven flew along behind him.

"Jonas, do you think the raven is Cecil? He is always around, and I think he is trying to help us. I feel like Alice must have felt when she met all of the strange characters in Wonderland. Surely you understood about that." He smiled.

We stopped again and sat on a nearby stump of a tree. Jonas seemed to be a bit sad. I wasn't sure I wanted to bother him but was really concerned about him. "Are you okay?" He remarked that he was a bit tired, and ready to move on. I thought he meant he wanted to just go ahead with our search, but I think he was really ready to go back to where he had been before coming to help us. I didn't ask him anything else.

I didn't want to think that we were lost, but Jonas chuckled. "Sometimes I get turned around, and I'm not sure in which direction we should be going. It must have something to do with my age." And he laughed again. "According to my built-in compass, we need to go this way." He pointed to the left and offered his arm. "Come, dear lady, we shall go off in search of the carousel."

I hadn't giggled in a long time but couldn't resist the urge. In fact, we skipped off and before long, we were standing in front of what remained of the old stables; a charred reminder of the fire. I asked if we could go inside and look around.

"Your wish is my command, princess, but we must be careful. That old wood isn't very reliable." *He bowed deeply.*

"I think the stable must have been elegant in its day because although the inside of the main building is burned, the character of the design is enchanting."

My goodness, where did that come from? I don't talk like that, do I?

Jonas noticed the change in my dialogue. "Should we have a bit of a look around?"

"Indeed, dear sir," I said, continuing the charade.

We pushed the large doors open, and there sitting on the floor was Matt looking very much like he had just awakened from a deep sleep. I had the immediate thought that I should have put a leash on him, to keep him close by.

"Matt, what are you doing here?"

"I was following the raven again and tripped over a big root or something and fell flat on my face." *He pointed to the dirt on his forehead and cheeks. "I couldn't get up for the longest time, and the next thing*

I knew, that stupid bird was pecking at me again. I didn't want him to get mad or anything, so I followed him and ended up here. It's a really neat place but all burned out. I actually saw horses in the stalls and heard them snorting and whinnying or whatever it is they do. It was almost real, but I saw that girl in the hat, and she pushed me down, and then you showed up. Why does she keep doing things like that? It was all too, too, too, too scary. I don't want to do anything on my own again. I promise I won't run off, and I'll stay right with you and Jonas. I'm going to have a lot to tell my folks when I get home. They'll never believe me."

So, it might be Daphne trying to keep us from reaching our goal. As I looked around the stable, I imagined real horses in the stalls; magnificent animals shook their heads up and down together directing me in a positive way. I'll show Daphne that she can't stop us! A new burst of enthusiasm spurred me on.

There were over two hundred acres to the property and thinking we would not have enough days to cover it all, I was worried. Not only that, but dark clouds had begun to move quickly in our direction, and in the distance, thunder rumbled. Summer storms come up all of a sudden in the South.

"Oh, piffle, now what do we do?"

Jonas answered my question. "I think that Matt

111

and you should head back to the house, so you don't worry your grandmother."

"What are you going to do? Do you want to go with us?"

"I still have my little house on the property. I will be perfectly safe there." In the blink of an eye, he was gone. Here we go again! That had been one of those 'occasional appearances' he had told us about earlier.

"Matt, hurry up, because we will get soaked if we don't reach the house before the sky opens up."

"You mean like in Chicken Little?" Matt grinned.

When I crossed my eyes at him, he said, "The sky is falling, the sky is falling." And he ran on ahead. Boy, I had fallen for that one. He slowed down and stayed pretty close to me, trying to keep up with his little legs.

Fifteen
Matt Gets His Wings

We were both out of breath and laughing when we reached the back porch. "I won," said Matt proudly.

My reply had been, "I let you win, Sherlock."

Grandmother was in the kitchen. We stepped inside just as the first crackle of thunder hit, and the sky opened up. The rain came down like someone had poured it from a big bucket and it smelled really good, but I still was disappointed that we hadn't been able to finish what we had wanted to accomplish that day. Oh, it had been exciting enough, for sure, and we had a lot to tell Grandmother, especially about Jonas.

She said, "I am glad you had the good sense to return before the storm," and gave both of us a big hug. "I'm sorry you didn't get to do more, but everything happens for a reason, and maybe tomorrow will be bright and sunny. Now, go get cleaned up before dinner, and then you can tell me all about your day. Did you eat the lunch I packed?"

"Oh, oh. I'm sorry, Aunt Bertie, but I guess I lost it when the raven attacked me. A lot happened to us

and eating was not first on our list of things to think about." He headed up to his room to clean up, and she looked at me with raised eyebrows, questioning that last remark.

"What did he mean that the raven attacked him? Is he okay?" She added, "He looked very dirty, but then, I guess little boys always get dirty."

"By the way," I asked, "how did Matt get here? I forgot to ask before. He lives in San Francisco, and I didn't see Uncle Cliff or Aunt Grace when he first got here."

Grandmother answered, "Since Matt considered himself old enough, and knowing that the stewardesses would watch him every step of the way, they agreed to let him fly by himself. It must have been quite an exciting trip for him. He took a cab here and, as they say, voila, there's Matt."

"I think he's a little creep. He never even told me. I've never gone anyplace by myself, and here little Matt travelled across the country by himself, and he isn't even eight yet! That's some kind of huge deal!"

"Crystal Elizabeth Baxter!"

Calling me by my full name, I knew Grandmother was disappointed. "Let me remind you that Mathew doesn't have half of the privileges you have. He lives in an apartment in San Francisco. He doesn't have a yard to play in. He can't have a dog because it's not allowed. He attends a very strict all boys' school. Do you understand what I'm saying?"

I reached over to my sweet grandmother and hugged her. "I feel so awful, and I am totally ashamed of myself. I didn't have any idea. No wonder he had been so willing to jump in and help. He needed to be noticed and wanted and appreciated. Well, I do appreciate him, and I really think he's a great kid, and so brave to make that plane trip all by himself. I promise that I will be sure to let him know how I feel. Thank you, Grandmother."

She sat very still and smiled, remembering how important it was to let those people we know and love just how important they are in our lives. She straightened her apron and continued preparing dinner. She raised her head and silently offered a prayer for her sweet granddaughter and grandnephew. "They are really good children, and I am very proud of them," she said, to no one in particular.

I had just stepped outside the kitchen door and overhead her words. It warmed my heart.

"Hey, Sherlock," I yelled, as I ran up the stairs. I did stop on the landing, however, to check out the stained-glass window. Flowers. That was good. "Where are you?"

"I'm in my room," he answered. "Is dinner ready? I didn't think I was hungry until I got out of the shower."

He started out the door, but I called to him. "Matt, wait a minute, I want to tell you something."

He came back into the room and leaned against the doorjamb. "Was Aunt Bertie mad because we didn't have lunch?"

"No, that's no biggie. I just wanted to let you know I think you are about the bravest person I know. How did it feel being on that big airplane and flying across the country all alone? Did you get a pair of wings? I heard they sometimes gave them to young, brave kids. May I see them, if you have them?"

Matt was so excited, he almost tripped over his own feet getting to the dresser where he had put his prized gift. "I know they are only plastic, but I felt like a real pilot when the stewardess pinned them on me. The pilot came back to see me later and shook my hand. I have never had anything that special happen to me – ever! I'll get to do it again when I go home. I was scared at first but didn't want to let my folks know. Anyway, it was more fun than I thought it would be. I got to read my comics and eat peanuts and a big meal, and when I got the wings, I was so proud. I just didn't want to brag, so I never told you. I thought you would make fun of me."

"Make fun of you? No way! I am very proud of you, and now I know why you are such a good assistant." I gave him a hug. "We should hurry downstairs. Grandmother has dinner almost ready, and then we'll need to go through everything we found out so far and plan what to do tomorrow. Maybe we'll go back to the attic and do some more exploring. There must be something else we've missed.

"Matt, tomorrow we should do what Hansel and Gretel did in the story, only instead of bread crumbs; we can tie strips of fabric on bushes to find our way back."

Matt liked the idea and called me 'boss' as he headed downstairs before me to see what had been making all those wonderful smells coming from the kitchen. I made a bet with myself that it was fried chicken.

I followed the aroma to the kitchen where Matt was – are you ready for this? – setting the table. Miracles did happen. Grandmother had fixed not only her famous fried chicken, but had fluffy mashed potatoes, gravy, fresh green beans, and the highest biscuits I had ever seen. And for dessert? Apple pie a la mode. What more could a couple of kids want?

"Grandmother, you're the best!"

She smiled and turned to Matt and winked. He was one happy camper.

Sixteen
Clues in the Attic

After dinner and cleaning up the dishes, Matt and I headed back toward the attic. The rain pounded the house, and Matt said, "We may have to build an ark to get to the other part of the property."

I had to laugh at that one but secretly agreed with him. We climbed the eight steps to the landing, and I automatically looked up at the stained-glass window. Oh, oh, the flowers had been replaced with the horse. I didn't say anything to Matt, but he saw me looking at the window.

"Weren't there flowers in that window before?" All I could do was shrug and nod. "Wow! Crazy – weird – strange. I love it!" Matt exclaimed.

We continued up the next eight steps to the second floor of the house and flipped on the hallway switch. I don't know why I had never noticed before but hanging on both sides of the hall were paintings of my ancestors. No, wait! They weren't there before. I tried to recall paintings of beautiful landscapes, and one that I especially remembered was a very colorful painting of a herd of wild mustangs. The detail of each horse was so real, I thought I could reach out and touch them. They were painted in full gallop, and the expressions on their faces were of total love for the feeling of being free. Leading the pack was a beautiful young colt. Where were all of those paintings? As I gazed upon the faces of people I had never met, I felt a connection, nevertheless. Should I go and tell Grandmother? Probably not, since by the time she got there, they would more than likely be gone.

Matt shook my arm and interrupted my thoughts. "Who are all those people? They look like the pictures in the albums. Have they always been hanging there? I don't remember seeing them before."

"They weren't there before." This was just another chapter in the strange mystery we were part of. The previous pictures had been replaced. I didn't know for how long, but at least we weren't bored.

We headed to the attic, being very careful because the switch wasn't easy to find in the dark. As we cautiously made our way up the sixteen steps, I felt along the wall for the switch I knew was there. At least, it used to be there. Where was it? Why couldn't I find the switch? Maybe we should turn around and head back downstairs. No sooner did I have that thought than the light went on all by itself. Matt had been following me closely, and I almost knocked him down the stairs when the light went on. I was startled.

119

Could you blame me? I didn't think I would ever get used to these strange happenings.

"Here we go again, Matt," I said. "We'll just have to pretend that all of these strange things are normal to us. If we continue to show we're afraid, whoever is doing all of those weird things will continue. If we act like these things happen every day, maybe they'll stop. Are you with me?"

"I'm definitely ready for whatever lies ahead, boss. What do you want me to do first; look in the trunks again? I wonder what more we have to find?"

I wasn't sure, but I didn't want to miss anything. Matt had found the boxes marked 'incantations' under the tray in the first trunk, so I guessed that maybe that would be a good place to start. There may have been other things in there. I asked him if he was game. I was sure he wanted in on everything, and his answer was, of course, "Yes."

We headed toward the first trunk when once again the lid opened by itself. I half expected it to do that and wasn't quite so shocked this time. I think I would have been disappointed, but it still creeped me out. How many kids ever got the chance to experience something like that? I took the tray out of the trunk and set it on the floor. The folders were still there, and we carefully took them out one at a time. They appeared to be in the same order as when Matt replaced them a few days before. We had only kept the one with the

120

seal. None of the rest of them had a seal like we had found on the one we took downstairs, and we felt we had the right one that would be a part of our puzzle.

Under the small boxes were stacks of letters, tied with colored ribbons. Matt was very animated as he pointed them out to me. "Look at these. I wonder if they are love letters."

I faced him with a questioning look. "What do you know about love letters? They might be but if they are, we shouldn't read them since they are very personal."

"Darn!" And then he laughed and said, "They are probably all mushy and stuff like that. Yuk."

"We should respect them and carefully put them away until we can see what else is in this trunk." He loved going through all the stuff. I said, "I bet that none of your friends back in San Francisco are doing what we are this summer."

"I am positively sure of that. By the way, have you gone through those other boxes and little trunks in the far corner of the attic?"

"Not yet. Can you slide one of them over to me?" The sound of rain on the tin roof and the distant thunder added to the drama of that evening. It was not just raining, it was pouring. Was it ever going to stop long enough for us to continue our search for the carousel?

"I think we need to check to see if there is

anything else that needs to be checked out in the open trunk first." Not finding anything that looked like it could have been part of what we were looking for, we put everything back. It was time to see what was in the other trunk, and I asked Matt if he could get it open. He was having problems with the latch.

"It won't open. Maybe you should call on somebody to help, like your great-grandmother, or one of your other ancestors. I bet there's someone sneaking around."

"I don't know if I can do that. We should continue; and maybe one of the smaller boxes will be easier to open. I wonder if there's a key to the trunk." I took one of the smaller boxes from Matt and sat down on the floor with it in front of us. Not sure as to what I might find, I slowly removed the lid. A pair of riding boots lay inside. "Oh, gosh; these must be Crystal Ann's. They're much too small for an adult. I feel like I am invading her privacy. I wonder if she was wearing them the day of the accident." A shiver traveled down my spine, and I gently replaced them and shut the box. Across the room, a vision of Michael sobbing appeared. My heart hurt for him. Then, he disappeared.

Another small box contained other personal possessions belonging to Crystal Ann, including her diary. I promised her out loud, "I won't look in it." I knew I would not want someone reading my private *thoughts. I gently placed the diary down and picked up a small jewelry box. I opened the top and sitting on a gold-colored pole was a carousel horse that turned around to the music that began to play when I opened the lid. It was the same music I had heard coming from the calliope. Inside were a few pieces of jewelry, including a ring with her birthstone. I knew that it was her birthstone, because our birthdays were in the same month – this month! In less than a week!*

I picked up a beautiful locket engraved on the outside with a fleur-de-lis. Matt asked, "What is that?"

"It's a French-stylized design of an iris flower." Did I say that? I had studied a lot of French history on my own at the library because of my heritage. That information must have stuck with me.

I knew my ancestors had come from France, but could they have been royalty? Grandmother had told me I had 'royal' features. I think they had first settled in Louisiana. When had they ended up in Georgia? More questions without answers; answers I will probably never know. Matt was impressed. "Open the locket and see if there are pictures in it."

I gently pushed the little clasp that held the locket pieces together, and inside were two tiny pictures; one of a baby (I assumed it was Crystal Ann) and a beautiful woman who had to be Emily, her mother. Wow, she looked just like my mother. Or at least, there was a strong family resemblance. I stared at those pictures for a long time, and was shaken from my temporary trance by Matt.

"Are you okay? You look like you have seen another ghost." Matt was concerned and mentioned that they must be pictures of Crystal Ann and her mother. "I've seen pictures of Aunt Margaret, and she looks a lot like her. That's amazing!"

Matt hit it right on the head. "Yeah," I said, "It is pretty amazing. It has brought me so much closer to everyone, holding that locket and seeing the pictures of the family I am trying to help. I have all kinds of unfamiliar emotions running through my mind. Are you feeling the same?"

"Yeah. What else is in the box?"

I placed the locket back in the jewelry case and fingered a little gold cross on a very fragile chain, and a tiny, thin gold bracelet that was probably her baby bracelet. I had one very much like that when I was about six months old. The music stopped when I closed the lid.

"Matt, what else do we have to look at?" He pointed to four other boxes in the corner. "And don't forget about the trunk that we can't unlock."

"You choose, Matt. We have lots of time unless the lights go out. The storm is getting pretty nasty." To take our minds off that, I told him to slide a box over to me.

This one was much larger than the ones I had looked in before, and I was anxious to see what it contained. I have to mention that these boxes were not your regular cardboard ones like we know today. These had lids instead of flaps, and some of them were oval-shaped with ribbons tied to keep the lid in place. They were decorated with flowers, kind of like wallpaper, and were very pretty. I was careful not to damage them.

Several beautiful hats, similar to the ones that my ancestor visions would wear, lay inside. I couldn't believe I was finding all of this stuff. They looked almost brand new. Each had been wrapped in a beautiful piece of fabric, I guess to keep them from dust. "How amazing is this! Matt, this is better than any museum we could have visited. Where can we see things like this and be able to actually touch them? I know these are all 'girl-type' things, but your history teacher would have loved them." He broke out in a big grin! I had touched a nerve. I grinned right back at him.

Just about that time, the lights began to flicker, and I hastily, but carefully, replaced the hats in the box and told Matt that we should slide those boxes back to the corner, and go downstairs. I wouldn't have been surprised if Grandmother called us any minute.

No sooner did I say that, than I heard that

familiar southern drawl calling us to come back downstairs right away. She had candles in case the power went off but reminded us that we wouldn't have any light up there. I looked at Matt, as we cautiously made our way down the sixteen steps.

Chloe listened intently over the rain and thunder, to hear if someone might be coming up the sixteen steps to get her. She was tired and hungry and very much alone. The storm showed no signs of letting up, and this was not where she wanted to spend the night.

"Grandma!" she yelled. But there was no answer.

Seventeen
Treasures from the Attic

"Grandmother, Matt found more boxes in the attic, and we opened three of them." After breathlessly bringing her up to date, Grandmother came over and put her arms around my shoulders.

I began to cry. "Grandmother, why did Crystal Ann have to die so young? She had her whole life ahead of her." Losing Mom and Dad when I did, had been the worst trauma of my life, but I had my grandmother, and that meant a lot. "And I saw Michael again right after I opened the box with Crystal Ann's riding boots. He was crying."

I had been so involved in trying to solve the mystery for Crystal Ann, that it had somewhat eased my pain. But it made me remember standing by the graves, realizing that my folks were gone, and I'd never see them again. I was determined to put all of the pieces of this puzzle together, so Crystal Ann could be with her folks again. "She never even got a chance to see her mother, once she was older. She only had the picture in her locket." I ran from the room up to my bedroom, crying.

Matt started after me, but Grandmother stopped him. "Just leave her alone for now." She told me later that he looked very sad because he hated to see me upset. They sat there for a long time listening to the rain on the tin roof and pretty soon, he calmed down. "Matt, now go upstairs and tell Crystal that we need to go through the things you found in the attic."

I was lying on my bed going over everything that had happened the past few days and silently prayed that the weather would clear up. I was so touched by the story about Crystal Ann's jewelry that I had forgotten to tell Grandmother about the hats. I planned to get up, wash my face, comb my hair, and go back downstairs when I heard a knock on the door.

"Hey, cuz, are you doing okay? Aunt Bertie said you should come back downstairs."

I walked over to Matt and put my arms around him. "I'm better than okay. I am the luckiest girl in the world to have a cousin like you and a grandmother like mine. I forgot to tell her about the hats and the locked trunk. We still have a lot to do, and I am ready for some more apple pie and ice cream. How about you?"

We both ran for the door at the same time and nearly got stuck in the threshold trying to get out. We both laughed so hard, we almost fell down. When we reached the landing, we looked up at the same time and gazed upon the carousel horse stained-glass window. Oh, boy!

Grandmother had already set out two plates for us. "Okay, my two detectives, it is time for us to go back into the front parlor and continue your 'mission'." The rain continued to pour with a vengeance, and it looked like it wasn't going to stop any time soon. The search for the carousel would have to wait until the weather cleared.

I asked her, "Where is the sealed incantation? I don't see it with all of the other stuff."

"I put it back in the trunk because I thought it would be safer there."

Matt and I both looked at her and Matt questioned her about going into the attic. "I thought you were afraid to go up there. Did you see anyone? Were you scared?"

"Slow down, Matt." I then turned to her. "Did you really go up there after all these years?"

"Whoa, you two! We all have fears we need to overcome, and it was because of two brave young people that I was able to go up there. I returned it to the trunk where you found it. As for seeing someone— " She paused, and we held our breaths. She continued, "I saw my mother. She came to me, just as Crystal Ann had appeared to you, Crystal."

"Wow! That's so neat." Matt was ready to hear more.

Eighteen
A Visit from Eunice

Relating to us what had happened that afternoon, Grandmother said she had gone into the attic looking for another clue, perhaps one that would hasten the process. I didn't remember her ever telling me that she had been up there before because she said it might not be safe. Actually, I think it was just a ruse to keep nosey kids out. Since I had gone up there a few times, and nothing happened, I guess she thought it was all right for her to go.

She began, "As I looked around the room, I was reminded of the days I spent there as a little girl with my friends. We used to play dress up with the clothes and hats and fans we found in the trunks and boxes. I don't remember ever seeing mannequins like you told me about and as much as I searched, I couldn't find them.

"I sat on the big cushion on the low stool and waited for something or someone to reveal itself to me. I was always very close to my mother, Eunice, and tried to will her to appear by thinking very strongly about her. Maybe she would have answers

to some of the questions that confronted me. It seemed like hours but was only a minute or two when I heard a soft, Southern voice, "Hell-o, my darling, Bertha. I am so glad to see you here. You are just as I had imagined you would be, still lovely."

Grandmother continued, "I looked around the room and there, in all of her loveliness, was my beautiful mother, standing by the window. She was dressed in a lovely long-sleeved blue gown with a high collar and lace on the bodice and cuffs. Pearl buttons adorned the front, and she carried a big hat with blue ribbons. I was stunned, but oh, so happy to see her. I smiled and said, 'Good afternoon, Mother. I have missed you so much and hoped you would come to me. I need some help with the mystery that Crystal is supposed to solve.' Then I repeated your story to her and told her that you had seen her and two of her sisters there a few days ago, and that you were quite amazed, to say the least. I asked her if she could make any sense of the things you had found. I said I knew I was talking way too much, but since that was the first time I had been able to talk to her, I didn't want to waste any time."

"Mother told me the following: 'Sweet Bertha, I haven't been able to use any of my craft for years – not until Crystal came up here and called out my name. She called me GG, which was really sweet. I finally figured out that she meant great-grandmother.

131

I like that. I made the trunk move and the lid open. I felt really good about that since I didn't know whether I still had it in me! But it worked. Gladys and Lucille were with me. The other sisters aren't into all of this reappearing stuff. They don't know what they are missing! I think this would be a wonderful time in which to live. I see you don't have to wear all of these heavy dresses and petticoats. As lovely as they are, I would much prefer the light house-dress you have on.'."

I composed myself. 'Mother, I want to help Crystal. When I told her about the visions and the journals and photos, one of the word phrases popped into my head and out of my mouth. I hadn't thought about it for over sixty years. How did I know it? What does it all mean, and how does it work together with the others Crystal found, to solve the mystery? Have I been talking too much?'

"My mother was smiling and shook her head, as she continued. 'You are still the sweet, compassionate little girl I remember, my dear; always wanting to help someone. Your sweet daughter, Margaret, was like that, too, and now I see the same character in our Crystal. I don't know what I can do, except what I have already done. She has the three sets of words now. The paper that reveals the pieces of the puzzle and the sealed envelope holds the incantation. I think there is one more piece needed to find the carousel. It

132

is in one of the remaining boxes and will reveal another secret about Crystal Ann and Michael's deaths.'

Bertie was so thrilled to be in contact with her mother, that she was overwhelmed. She heaved a big sigh and straightened the front of her apron with her hands.

Her mother had continued. 'The raven is a part of this, but I'm not sure in what capacity, and now Crystal needs to find the carousel. You must show her the map of the property where the pavilion is located. Look through your important papers for the map is key to finding it. How she puts it all together is what will make it work.'

Eunice had repeated everything that we all knew, and Grandmother was excited that she had learned something new – the secret about Crystal Ann and Michael's deaths.

"I turned to say something to my mother, but she was gone. On the floor where she had been standing was a small piece of the blue ribbon from her hat. I picked it up and tied to the end was a small, odd-shaped key. What it unlocks is just another hurdle we have to cross. All in all, it was so wonderful to see my sweet mother again."

She had a wistful look in her eyes, sort of between sad and happy. "Now all we have to do is figure out what the key unlocks." She said she looked *all around the attic and didn't see anything that had a lock on it.*

"Mother, please come back, I need you again." But there was nothing. No sound. No sweet velvet, southern drawl. She was all alone in the attic pondering what to do next.

When she was a little girl, Grandmother used to keep a diary. It still sat on her nightstand, where it had been ever since she had moved back into the house. But she thought, "I have the key to it in my jewelry box, don't I? Maybe this key has nothing to do with anything. Maybe she just dropped it accidentally. Yes, that's it! Well, as they say, all will be revealed." Not knowing whether she had helped me or not, she headed toward the door, took one last look around, and slowly closed the door behind her. She secretly hoped that we were having better luck than she had.

Stepping outside of her mental journey, Chloe set the journal on her lap and recapped what she had just learned. She was anxious to get out of the attic. It was getting dark, and she had to pee. Will anyone ever find her? Did anyone care? Will she die up there and become another ghost in the attic? If only her grandma could appear like Eunice had if she asked for her. But she's not dead! She made a promise to herself to be better if she ever got out. Well, it wasn't like she was in prison, and her life wasn't so miserable after all. She tried the door again. Still locked. She *was* in prison! After thinking about things, though, Chloe decided that her grandma's house wasn't all that bad, in fact, it was very comfortable and 'homey'. She especially loved the big bed in her room with the high canopy. Arranged on top of the bedspread were soft pillows of different sizes covered in colorful prints. It was a comfortable room, and she wished that she were there now.

She had been complaining about how she couldn't go anywhere, got angry, and ended up locked in like a criminal. It was like she had given herself a time out. She had time to think. Her grandma's story was making her realize how much we all needed each other and how she had taken her mom, her dad, and her grandma for granted.

Chloe resolved to be better if only someone would open the door and let her out. She banged on the door, but there was no response. She opened the tin box of candles and lit a match. Dripping a little wax onto the top of the tin lid, she set the candle in the melted wax and steadied it up so it wouldn't fall. She might as well keep on reading and once again she was back in time.

Nineteen
More Treasures

"Grandmother, we tried to open another one of the trunks, but it was locked. Do you think that maybe that key will fit the trunk? Maybe that's why your mother left it for you." We were getting all kinds of help, I thought, and touched my necklace, silently asking for the key to work. Grandmother agreed that we would go to the attic the next morning. However, at that moment, there were other things we needed to talk about.

When I told her about the beautiful hats, she said, "I wouldn't be a bit surprised if they belonged to Great-Grandmother Eunice, and her sisters. Back in those days, people took such pride in everything they did and cared about what they had. That's why the hats are in such good shape today. We should all take care of our things, and then someday they can be passed on to others to enjoy."

"I understood. Remember that you had told me once about the needlepoint and making things of the period that reflected what the family was? I didn't completely get it before, but I do now."

Matt had been very quiet, but then said, "I don't think my dad has anything in his garage that would mean anything to members of future generations of our family. My family doesn't do a lot of neat things like your ancestors used to do."

I walked over to Matt and put my hand on his shoulder. "Maybe we, personally, don't have needlepoint and old hats and things like that to leave behind, but our generation will go to the moon and develop all sorts of amazing electronic things that our ancestors couldn't have even dreamed about. We are finding cures for diseases that used to kill people at a very young age a hundred or so years ago. And the pictures we leave in albums will be just as important to our children and grandchildren and on down the line, as those we found in the attic. Just because we don't do needlepoint; we aren't any less important than they were."

"You said a mouthful, Crystal," Matt replied. "I guess I hadn't thought about it like that. Okay, so what's next?"

Grandmother had a big smile on her face. Matt certainly had a way of putting everything into perspective.

I related our day with Jonas. She asked us whether we thought she should meet Jonas. She didn't like the idea of us running around with someone she didn't know.

I understood what she was saying, but I said, "I didn't know Crystal Ann or the raven, and you haven't been worried about my running around with them! If Jonas could help us solve the mystery, that would be wonderful. And, since he used to live on the estate, he knows the property like the palm of his hand. He has already helped us, and I just know he isn't going to let anything happen to us. I'll ask him to come back with us tomorrow to meet you, and you can see for yourself." I just hoped that the rain would ease up, so we could get back outside.

She agreed. "Yes, you should bring him back with you, and I will hear what he has to say. I have many questions, but very few answers at this point. I know you won't do anything dangerous, and I pray that Jonas will be the friend you believe him to be. I will try to find the map of the adjoining property, so you will have that information to guide you in the right direction. For now, I have a lot of thinking and doing to do."

Twenty
Restless Night and French Toast

It rained all night long, and I kept waking up from dreams that were very confusing. Everyone was present; my folks, Matt, Jonas, Crystal Ann, Michael, and Grandmother. The raven kept flapping his wings and at one time, tried to sit on my shoulder, as if to stop me from doing something. The calliope music sounded louder than ever, and I could see the carousel spinning round and round, and once again, I ended up on the floor. This had to stop!

The next morning dawned with fluffy clouds against a clear blue sky. I jumped up and opened the shades and window letting in the fresh smell of the day. I loved the weather after a good rain. Granted, it was humid in Georgia, but today I didn't care. This was going to be a great day!

I showered, made my bed, and dressed. I remembered I had to get some old pieces of fabric or rags to tie on bushes as we headed to the back of the property, so we could find our way back. Grandmother had a sewing basket that she kept in the linen closet, and I set out to look for it. I ran smack into Matt as he was coming out of his room. He must have been having the same thoughts about the 'Hansel and Gretel' thing. "Are you going to get something to tie on the trees and bushes?"

"Great minds always run along the same track. And a good morning to you, Sherlock. I was heading for Grandmother's sewing basket. Are you ready for a good day?"

In true Matt fashion, he said, "You betcha. I didn't sleep very well, though. I kept dreaming about everything we have been doing and woke up several times. One time, I couldn't remember where I was. Is that crazy?"

"I assure you that it isn't crazy at all. I had the same kind of night. Maybe it's because we have so little time left. Jonas did tell me that we would get everything accomplished and have time to spare. I hope he's right."

"I want it all done before I have to go home. I don't want to miss out on the big day."

Trying to assure Matt I said, "Remember that Jonas said we will finish in time, so I think your chances of being a part of the big day, as you put it, are pretty good."

We headed off to find Grandmother. We both looked up at the same time to see the horse in the stained-glass window was still there. Matt looked at me, and I think we both had the same thought. Maybe that was a good sign.

Grandmother was busy preparing bacon and French toast, one of my very favorites. She didn't just use plain bread, but bread she had baked herself and cut very thick before she worked her 'magic' on each slice. Not only were the slices dipped in egg, but she used a little sugar and cinnamon, too. One piece was all I could eat, but I enjoyed every bite.

Matt outdid me with the French toast and had two slices. Surprise, surprise! "I'll have to tell Mom about this, so she can make it exactly the same as you did, Aunt Bertie." After gulping down a big glass of milk, he asked her if she had any old pieces of rags we could use to tie on bushes on our way to the back of the property. "Crystal thought if we did that, we won't get lost on our way back."

Smiling broadly, she replied, "I think I can find something. It's really a good idea. It reminds me of the story, Hansel and Gretel." Matt and I both chuckled, as I handed her the sewing kit. She also pulled an old rolled up map from her apron pocket and handed it to me.

"Crystal, I think this will be a big help to you. When mother mentioned that there was a map of the property, I spent hours last night looking through all of the papers I could find, and there it was, in the back of the top drawer of that old desk in the back parlor."

As we unrolled the map, we saw an "x" showing

the location of the house; another for the carriage house; one for the stables, and a curved line that looked like it could be a road, or a path, leading to the other piece of property. There were other markings on the map, too. A square with what looked like crosses showed the family cemetery. This could be a very interesting day to be sure. I rolled up the map and put it in my back pocket. I felt that we were finally headed in the right direction.

"Grandmother, thank you. I'm sure this will help us. But the other property is so big, how will we ever be able to find the carousel in time?"

"Just use your instincts. Keep track of your time and be back before dark. And one other thing; remember to bring Jonas back so I can meet him. I'll keep good thoughts for you to have a wonderful, successful day. I made you a little snack in case you get hungry. Matt, put it in your backpack so you don't lose it. Now, be on your way. Crystal, do you have your watch?"

I assured her I did. It was a sporty waterproof-type watch that my dad had given me when I was ten. Matt and I kissed Grandmother, and she waved to us as we set out on another search for the carousel. We had put the tools back in the shed and stopped there to pick them up. The door was easy to open this time, and it appeared that everything was just as we had left it two days before. So far, so good, I thought, as I closed the door behind us on our way out, armed with a shovel and rake.

We walked along, checked the map, talked about our adventure, and stopped ever so often to tie a piece of fabric on a bush. "I wonder where Jonas is." Just as I had that thought, there he was, standing in the middle of the path, armed with a long piece of rope and a big knife. He startled us, and I immediately had a scary thought that maybe he wasn't our friend, as Grandmother had questioned, and maybe he planned to do something bad to us with that rope and knife. Matt looked at me as if to say something, but Jonas interrupted us.

"Did I startle you? I didn't mean to."

I pointed to the rope and knife, and said, "It was just that my mind jumped to all kinds of conclusions, and I couldn't imagine what you might do with those."

Looking embarrassed, Jonas said, "I am so sorry I scared you. The knife is to cut away any weeds we may find, and the rope is to tie around large roots, in order to pull them away. I'm sure there is a lot of kudzu and weeds and vines covering the carousel enclosure, and since we don't have any machinery to work with, we will have to use our own methods to remove whatever is there. I assure you that I would never hurt you and won't let anyone else hurt you either."

We both ran to Jonas and hugged him. We were

relieved, of course, to know that he hadn't planned anything evil. In fact, I thought it might be a good time to mention it to him. "Grandmother will love you as much as we do and will be happy to know that you have been taking such good care of us. So, what do you think about that? Will you go back with us?"

Jonas tipped his cap, bowing slightly, and said, "Dear lady, I would consider it a pleasure. Now, let's be on our way, or the day will be over before we begin."

I showed him the map, and after looking it over, he replaced his cap and turned toward the back of the property, beckoning us to follow. I was sure that would be the best day we would have, and Matt grinned from ear to ear.

Twenty-One
The Raven Shows the Way

As we walked along what used to be a path but was now a muddy river after the past rain, Matt tied pieces of the fabric to several bushes. He realized what an important job this was and did it seriously. I was very glad Matt was there to be a part of my journey. He had become a close friend, as well as being my cousin, and I knew I would miss him when he left.

We passed the burned-out stables that had been the farthest we had gone away from the main house.

I turned to Matt, "Do you recall where you were when you thought you saw the carousel?"

Matt stopped next to me. "I had been running, following the raven. I wasn't really paying attention to where I was, and now, since the rain, everything looks so different." He lowered his head, looking very sad. "I'm sorry."

I walked over to him. "It's all right. We'll find it. We have Jonas now, and since he had lived here, surely, he will know where it was. Right, Jonas? Jonas, where are you?"

Okay, this wasn't what he was supposed to be doing. He was supposed to be watching after us, not running off.

Matt and I sat on a couple of big logs alongside the path and waited. A few minutes passed when the raven appeared and alighted right next to Matt, who was startled, to say the least. The raven sat very still and that was different for him, since he usually was very animated. Matt held out his hand slowly toward the raven. I wanted to be ready to jump in if I needed to but remained very quiet.

Matt asked the raven if he could please show us where the carousel was. He told him we weren't afraid of him, but we needed to find it to help solve a big mystery. "Do you understand me?" Matt asked the raven. Then, Matt said, "He must understand because he has been a big part of this whole thing from the beginning."

The black raven – and I had to remind myself that he was a 'bird' – nodded his head, jumped down off the log, and hopped a few feet in the direction we had been headed. Matt and I looked at one another but didn't say anything. As if he had read my mind, Matt tied another piece of fabric to a bush before we started to follow the raven. Just then, Jonas reappeared, and the raven flew off.

Matt threw a handful of fabric strips to the ground in frustration and turned to Jonas. "The raven was about to show us where the carousel is, and you scared him off!" I thought he was going to cry, but he didn't. Instead, he said, "I'm sorry, Jonas. This is all just so weird."

Feeling badly himself, Jonas said, "I'm so sorry I scared off the raven, but I am sure we are headed in the right direction. I had gone on ahead in order to be sure there weren't any big mud holes or animals that might get in our way."

"Jonas, I'm sorry, too, but it was just that I wanted so much to have the raven show us the way. He was very friendly and didn't peck on my cap like he had done before."

All of our hard efforts looked like they were going to pay off. Knowing that the deadline was quickly approaching, I needed for this revelation to be true and not just another false alarm. Matt was excited. "Come on, let's go!"

We must have looked funny to anyone not knowing what we were doing. Two kids and a man over a hundred years old, cautiously making their way in search of a mystical place over two hundred years old, stopping ever so often to tie pieces of fabric on half-dead bushes or fallen trees. It sounded like something from a fairy tale. Following the map, we ventured deeper into the adjoining property, carefully marking our route.

We had been walking for over half an hour and

Jonas pointed out a little house. "That's where my family lived. It's almost like it was when I lived there before. The walls and floors are a little creaky, but so am I!"

I related to Matt the fact that Jonas and his family had been slaves. "This just gets better as we go along," was Matt's reply.

Jonas laughed, and before we could say anything, he said he didn't think it was a good idea for us to go in there. We had bigger fish to fry, as they say. We had to find our treasure and return to the house before dark.

Off to the right a small cemetery surrounded by a low fence came into our view. "Look! Let's check this out!" I ran over to the fence and turned around in time to see Jonas and Matt approaching. The raven was sitting on top of the fence and bobbed his head as I approached. He always seemed to be around.

Knowing that this was sacred ground, I held onto my crystal horse as memories of my parents' funeral came flooding back. Matt came up to me and held my hand. "Crystal, I think I know how you are feeling, and we don't have to stay here if you don't want to."

"No, I want to see whose graves are here. Thank you for being so caring. Jonas, do you remember anything about these graves?"

"Yes, Miss Crystal, I do. I wasn't sure they were still uncovered because no one ever came up here

once the house was closed up. There were just too many memories and too much sadness, and there was no one left to take care of them."

I approached the markers and the first one read, 'Emily Ann Le Grande, beloved mother and wife'. That was Crystal Ann's mother. Next to her grave was a beautifully hand-carved wooden cross, on which was inscribed 'Crystal Ann Le Grande, my precious daughter'. The third marker was for Michael, and the words were carefully carved into the stone: 'Michael Evan Le Grande, beloved father and husband.' In another area of the cemetery we found headstones for all of my relatives who had lived and died on the estate. One more headstone stood all by itself in a far corner of the cemetery. I walked toward it, wondering whose it could be. Matt was still holding my hand and standing beside the headstone when we read the inscription: 'Daphne'. Why doesn't she have a last name? Is she the same Daphne that you were talking about, Jonas?"

Jonas removed his hat and scratched his head. " Crystal Ann's friend was named Daphne. She was a pretty girl. Crystal Ann took a liking to her because no one else would. She was killed in the fire at the stables. No one knew if she had a family, because she never said, so we buried her here. I have forgotten why she was in the stables that day. People speculated that she had started the fire, but no one

149

could prove it. After Crystal Ann died, she used to come around to talk to Michael, but he didn't seem to want to have anything to do with her. It's a mystery we may never get answers to."

As I looked back toward the other graves, I saw a vision of Michael, holding his hands out to me in a pleading manner once again, and then he faded away.

"Jonas, there is so much more to find out. We need to hurry along now. Matt, be sure to mark this cemetery so after all of this is over, we can clean up the area to show respect for those who are buried here." My emotions were very high at that moment, and I wanted to cry, but didn't. "Jonas, which way do we go?"

"My head is telling me to go one way, but my heart is saying go another way." He pointed to the left. "My memory isn't so very good today for some reason. It's almost like part of it has been erased. I knew yesterday but I am foggy today. I didn't sleep very well last night."

"We'd better look at the map again," I said. The cemetery had been clearly marked. "Keep tying pieces of fabric on the bushes, Matt."

As Matt and I stayed close to each other, we kept looking around in case Daphne was following us or hiding in the woods, right where we were. Would she hurt us? I wondered.

On we walked for what seemed like miles although I knew it was only a few hundred yards. The raven was sitting on the stump of a giant oak doing his wing flapping thing, and jumping up and down. As we approached the stump, the raven hopped to the ground. He cocked his head at me, almost beckoning. Poking around the stump with the shovel, I hit something hard. Pulling away some thorny vines, I found the cornerstone of a building marked 1855. "It's the carousel house!"

"Wow," said Matt. "I guess where I thought it was, wasn't." He clapped his hands and laughed.

Matt, Jonas, and I thrashed at the vines. The raven shrieked as if to cheer us on. It was an impossible task and there was mud everywhere. We must have been at it for an hour and hadn't made any headway. My hands were cut from the thorny vines; I was full of mud, and my back hurt. I couldn't see how in the world we were going to be able to clear away that entire thicket. Now that we had found what we were looking for, we were not about to give up.

Standing about twenty feet away from where I was, a fuzzy vision of an angry Daphne appeared. She threw her hat on the ground in a defiant manner, and I saw her disfigured face and my heart broke. "Daphne, why are you so mad? Talk to us." But Daphne faded away and left me with no answers. It was getting late, and if we didn't leave right away, we

151

wouldn't be back by six like I had promised Grandmother. At least we knew where to start looking the next day. I was so excited! Urging Matt and Jonas on, I said, "We need to hurry and get back, so we can tell Grandmother the good news. Jonas, remember that you are coming to the house to meet her."

Jonas said, "I wouldn't miss it." He had a big grin on his face that looked like he had just opened a favorite Christmas present.

Matt was sure he wouldn't sleep that night; he was so excited about everything. Our search was almost over, but he reminded himself that they had promised Aunt Bertie they would be back by six, and a promise was a promise. We were not going to go against Grandmother's wishes.

Tossing my head in his direction, calling him Sherlock, I started to run, telling him that I would race them to the house. And off we ran, following the scraps of material.

Twenty-Two
Jonas Meets Bertie

Matt won the race and told us that we were just not fast enough to beat the champ. He stepped on the bottom step to the back porch just ahead of me. I said I didn't mind coming in second but didn't add that I had let him win. He was so proud of himself. Jonas toddled along behind, arriving a few minutes later. As we climbed up the porch steps, I reminded Matt and Jonas to take off their muddy shoes because we would really be in trouble if we tracked in mud.

Always the gentleman, Jonas tipped his hat and said, "Yes ma'am, Miss Crystal." I liked it when he called me that.

Jonas added, "I am afraid I don't look right to meet your grandmother. My clothes aren't tidy, and I don't have my shoes on. Michael always insisted on my looking presentable when greeting young ladies."

I smiled at the remark about young ladies but didn't say anything. "Don't be silly, Jonas. Grandmother will be very happy to meet you regardless of what you look like."

In the mudroom, just inside of the porch, Matt

took great pleasure in showing Jonas how to turn on the faucets. He was so excited to see the water come out! This was a new experience for him. The room was made just for what we were doing, and I said I didn't think it was there when he was around. Matt offered to show him all of the plumbing after dinner. I looked at Jonas out of the corner of my eye, and he was noticeably nervous, but still had a twinkle in his eye.

"Come on, it'll be fine. Matt, are you cleaned up?"

"Right-o, Miss Crystal," he said, copying the way Jonas had said my name. "Let's go in. I smell something wonderful."

She was standing at the stove, stirring something in a pot. Wearing her ever-present apron, she was a vision of the perfect grandmother.

I was sure to point out to her as we entered the kitchen, that we had arrived on time, and repeated Matt's observation that something smelled great. I introduced Jonas to her, and he had her charmed right away, giving a low half-bow in her direction.

"It's a pleasure to meet you, ma'am. I can see where Miss Crystal gets her beauty." I think I saw her blush. I know I did.

"It is indeed a pleasure to meet you. Thank you for all of your help with our project. Crystal told me how nice you have been, and I hope you like roast beef." With a little grin, she admitted, "I am semi-

famous for my pot roast and biscuits." That was an understatement. "Of course, that's only within our family."

Jonas replied, "I enjoyed many wonderful meals in this house cooked by your great-grandmother. You come by it naturally."

"Matt, your mouth is open; did you want to say something?" she asked.

"This is just all too strange. Here we are, about to have dinner with a man who is over a hundred years old, and it all seems so normal. No one will ever believe me," was his answer.

I remember Jonas' reply as if it was happening right now. "I am rather surprised, too, Matt, but have always been of the thinking that things happen for a reason in the way they are supposed to happen. The only thing is that I can't stay here past dark. I have to be back at my house before that. When we are allowed to come into this time, there are rules we have to follow in order to stay for a short period. And, I am so happy that I am allowed to eat your wonderful food."

We sat at the big table where Grandmother had set four places for dinner and suggested that we began dinner right away. She mentioned that one of the good things about that time of year – the summer – was that it didn't get really dark until around eight, so he would have time to enjoy a good dinner and return on time.

The dinner was wonderful, and the conversation revolved around the carousel and how we were going to remove all of the heavy branches and weeds that surrounded the enclosure. Since time was of the essence, we had agreed to meet at the location at six-thirty the next morning. We would bring all of the tools we could find, wear gloves, long sleeves, and hats to protect us from getting scratched or bitten by the many bugs that inhabited the property.

Jonas ate a hearty dinner, said his thanks, and at seven-thirty, he left. "I'll have to look at the plumbing some other time, Matt."

We all said goodbye and stood at the back door. Jonas got as far as the tool shed and disappeared into thin air. We shook our heads at the scene we just witnessed.

"Pinch me, I'm dreaming. How could he be here, a real person, and then just disappear into nothing?" Matt's question was on my mind as well.

Grandmother tried to explain in a way to keep us focused. "Jonas is a spirit similar to the ones that you and I had seen, Crystal, but in a more solid form to keep our minds focused on the job at hand. Certain spirits are allowed to come to us in that fashion but may not stay in that form when it gets dark. My mother and aunts are in a different spirit state. They have already made the completion but can return from time to time when they are needed. Crystal Ann, on the other hand, is incomplete. That is what you and Crystal and all of our helpers are working toward. Matt, do you understand?"

"Oh, yeah, sure," he said. And then in typical Mathew style, he said, "I'm going to go read some of my comic books and clear my head. There's nothing like Dick Tracy to get a boy thinking right."

Trying to keep a straight face, Grandmother told him to go ahead and be sure to take a shower before he went to bed. Matt ran to Grandmother and hugged her tightly.

I admitted that everything had been a lot for a little guy to understand, and I wasn't sure I totally understood all that had been going on that week, either. The next day could be a red-letter day, as they say. We had found the cornerstone of the carousel house, and it was my hope that we would be able to find someone with heavy equipment to remove all of the weeds and vines and stuff that covered it. I hoped that Michael knew that we were doing this because Crystal Ann had asked me to. Seeing Michael at the site made me believe that he knew I could help him.

Now it was time for my hug. Grandmother came over to me, wrapped her arms around me, sat down in a chair, and pulled me into her lap. I felt her gently rocking and she sang a song she used to sing to me when I was very little. I calmed down and knew I was on the right track to solving this mystery.

She assured me that I was equal to the task ahead. I wanted to share everything with my parents, but they weren't there anymore. We had always worked out problems together. I wished I could make them materialize. I was nervous and exhausted.

She said, "Matt will be fine. Dick Tracy will bring him back to reality." She laughed a little, and I got her meaning. "Go up and take a long, hot bubble bath. You will feel a lot better."

I asked her if she wanted some help with cleaning up, but she said she could do it quickly and then was going to read for a while.

I looked in on Matt on my way upstairs. As I passed the back parlor, there he was sound asleep on the couch. Dick Tracy was on the floor, creating a contrast to the little boy who looked every bit the innocent child. I was really going to miss him. Why had I been mean to him so many times before when we were together? Looking at him for a minute, I decided to let Grandmother wake him to take his shower. With that thought, I headed up the stairway, stopped on the landing, and said goodnight to the carousel horse in the stained glass.

Twenty-Three
Hansel and Gretel Get Lost

After my bath, I dried and brushed my unruly hair, and pulled back the covers ready for a good night's sleep. What was that noise? Oh, no, not again! Was the rain ever going to go away?

That night the skies were bright with lightning and the air trembled with thunder. I fell asleep to its symphony and dreams of my parents and the raven. My parents were standing together, showing me that they were with me. The raven was hopping around frantically, awkwardly flapping his wings. An old woman cloaked in a hooded garment told the raven he would learn the hard way what black magic could do as punishment for his transgression.

The raven squawked at her in supplication, but she disappeared into the fog. I had so wanted to have a restful sleep. What in the world was going on? I tossed and turned, not understanding what all of that was about.

When I woke up the next morning at six, I lay in bed for a few minutes and strained to hear if it was still raining. No sound of raindrops. That was good.

I got up to see the sun on its way to greeting the morning, and I silently said a thank you prayer. I was sure that day was going to be special, in spite of the dream. I'd try to forget about it, because I was on a mission. I didn't hear anyone stirring and hoped that Matt remembered we were leaving at six-thirty.

I walked down to Matt's room, gently knocked on the door, and called out quietly to see if he was up. No response. I knocked again and felt someone was standing behind me. When I turned, I gave out with a scream. There stood Matt, a half-eaten banana in his hand, a pair of gloves sticking out of his back pocket. His hair was tousled like he hadn't slept well or hadn't combed his hair yet.

"You scared me, Matt. How long have you been up? Your hair is all messed up."

"Whoa! Calm down, Crystal. I just got up a few minutes ago and was hungry, so I went downstairs to get something. I'm barely awake, but I promise I'll be ready to go in a few minutes with my hair combed and my bed made."

"I'm sorry; I didn't mean to jump on you. It's just that the time is closing in on us, and it stormed all night, and I had a weird dream, and – may I have a bite of your banana?"

He handed it to me. "Don't eat it all. Aunt Bertie is making breakfast. I'll be down in a few minutes."

I returned to my room and slipped on a pair of

jeans and two pairs of socks. I figured they would give me more protection against stickers or thorns or whatever else may be under those vines. Since I was going to wear a T-shirt with long sleeves, I picked one with a high neck, too. I put on my treasured necklace and stuck it inside of my shirt. I needed to wear it, but I didn't want to lose it. Looking around the room, I heaved a big sigh and headed off to what I was sure was going to be a successful day.

Grandmother was an incredible person, always doing things for others. At that moment, I was reminded of how much I loved her. When I entered the kitchen, she turned toward me. "When I heard the storm, I didn't know what to expect this morning. But it looks like it has passed us by. There will still be lots of mud out there, so please be careful."

I promised we would. "Do you know how much I love you?" I gave her a big hug and kissed her on the cheek. "Do you want to go with us? It would be wonderful if you could see us uncover the carousel."

She begged off. "It's a bit farther than I want to walk, and I plan to have dinner ready when you got back. Then Matt and you can tell me all about your day." With that, she turned back to the stove, just as Matt walked into the room.

"Oh boy, waffles and ham! Yummy. I sure like this restaurant." And he laughed his loud guffaw, as he filled his mouth with walnut waffles topped with

whipped butter and warm maple syrup.

"Be sure to leave a big tip," she said, and then added, "Tell Jonas to take special care of my special kids. Now, go along with you, and don't be late coming home."

We headed to the mudroom and turned to wave at her. At that very moment, I thought I saw my mother standing next to her.

"Matt, did you see that? I could swear I saw my mother standing next to Grandmother."

Cocking his head to one side, he asked me if I was sure. A lot had been going on lately, and maybe it was just my imagination. "That would be pretty neat though, if it really was Aunt Margaret. I wish I had seen her."

We sat on the steps of the mudroom and put on our shoes. They were still pretty much covered with mud. No sense in cleaning them up, because they were only going to get muddy again. I did, however, shake them down pretty good, in case some critter had decided to make them its motel. I warned Matt about it, too, and he rolled his eyes, but I noticed he checked the inside of each shoe.

"Okay, Hansel, let's go find our trail signs." We found the pieces of fabric along the way, even though they were pretty soaked from the previous night's storm. I was so glad we had done that, if I do say so myself.

In about an hour, we had made pretty good progress. We had picked up tools from the tool shed; stopped for a minute at the stables to see if there was anything there we could use, and slowly made our way through the area of the property that didn't really have a path. I was concerned. "I thought we had trampled down the weeds flat enough each time we came out here, but the rain and wind from the last night's storm have made all of these small trees fall across the direction we were heading. Now, where is the next piece of fabric?" I must have looked perplexed because Matt asked if we were lost.

"No, we're not lost." But honestly, I wasn't sure. Okay, the whole point in tying fabric to bushes and trees was so we wouldn't get lost. Piffle! I looked back in the direction we had come from and in the distance saw a bright yellow piece of fabric. That was a good sign. "Let's move a couple of these newly fallen small trees to see if there actually is a path underneath." When we did, all we saw was more brush. There was no way we could clear all of that away. Which way were we supposed to go now? I didn't see any more signs of fabric, and I was sure we were really, really lost. I called out, "Jonas, can you hear us?" If he did, he could come to us.

Matt was all for that, and we both hollered, "Jonas! Jonas! Where are you?" We were quiet for a minute and then repeated our call. I didn't want to get *lost in all of this unfamiliar territory and chose to stay where we were, hoping that Jonas or maybe even the raven would hear us. I was not in favor of moving from this spot unless I knew we were heading in the right direction. We might go twenty or thirty feet in any direction, but we didn't know what last night's storm might have brought in.*

The sound of calliope music filled the air. Wow, all we had to do was follow it, and we would be there. I asked Matt if he heard the music and if he could tell where it was coming from.

"I don't hear anything, Crystal. Are you okay?"

Oh, swell, that wasn't a good thing. Was I the only one who heard the music? "Matt, I heard music, just like I had in the past. Let's follow it. Come on, let's go."

Matt hollered at me. "Following the music will get us lost, and what you hear is only in your head, and—"

"Are you coming or not? We have to find the carousel. I don't mean to be so tough, but we are running out of time, and I have to believe that it must be in the direction of the music I am hearing. In fact, it is so loud; I can't believe you don't hear it."

I had gone about fifty feet or so and looked around and saw that Matt was still standing where we had been before. What was I going to do now? He was my responsibility, and I just couldn't leave him

164

*there. I walked back to where he stood, looking so
forlorn. "I am sorry I was rough on you, but we need
to get all of those weeds and things cleared away so
we can do whatever it is we are supposed to do next.
It is important that you are with me. I need your help.
I assure you that I'm not nuts. I did hear the music. I
don't know why I am the only one who can, but we
must press on. I can't do this without you."*

*Those must have been the magic words because
he gave me a hug, and said, "Okay, boss, let's go. But
you have to lead the way because I don't hear the
music."*

*We walked slowly, looking for pieces of fabric
tied to the bushes. A rabbit ran across our path, and
Matt squealed when he almost stepped on him. Then
he squealed again when he found a piece of cloth. We
were going in the right direction. I was happy about
that.*

*Little by little, we worked our way in the
direction of the music and found more signs showing
the way. This had gotten more exciting as we went
along. My mind raced in time to the music, and I
looked at Matt who had cocked his head in the
direction we were walking and said, "I hear it,
Crystal. I hear the music." He ran ahead of me
straight into Jonas who was coming toward us.*

*"Hey, little man, where are you going in such a
hurry? I've been waiting for both of you and was*

getting worried. I feel much better now that you're here."

Words tumbled out of my mouth. "I kept hearing the music and thought if we followed the music we'd make it sooner or later. Do you hear the music? Of course, you do. At first, Matt said he didn't hear the music, but now he does."

Both Matt and Jonas laughed at me, and it was so funny, I had to laugh, too. Well, that was a relief. Grandmother always told me it was good to laugh. She was right again.

More determined than ever, I asked, "Jonas, can we go now? Can you lead us? Like yesterday? There is a lot of work to do, clearing away all of the brush and vines. I have brought the tools and with the rope you have and – what?" I hadn't gotten any reaction except that he was smiling. "I mean it; we need to get that job done today if we can."

"Turn to your left, and you will see where we were yesterday at the cornerstone of the building."

There in front of us was the big mess of greenery we had seen yesterday. I had so hoped somehow it would have all been cleared away, but that was not to be. I was just very happy to be at our destination.

"Okay, let's get busy!" Matt was ready to tackle the huge undertaking and had a big rake in his hand. "Are you with me, you two?"

"You bet, Sherlock, let's clear away this mess!"

was my reply.

I turned to see Daphne standing near the thicket, gesturing that she was angry that we were there. I was not going to let her get the best of me, though. I was on a very important mission. I told her to go away, that she had no power over me, and I was going to complete what I started. Not waiting to see whether she was still around, I put on my gloves and began pulling at the weeds that had covered up Michael's dream. "We will do this!"

Hours flew by, and Matt and Jonas had a sort of assembly line thing going. Jonas pulled away roots and weeds with the piece of rope he had brought, handing them off to Matt, who threw them into a big pile away from the pavilion. He was so little and was doing such a big job.

He eventually sat on a nearby stump and said, "I don't know how much more I can do today."

I chopped at vines and swatted mosquitoes and other bugs and looked out for snakes and other critters. It was around three in the afternoon when I said, "We have to keep going. We can't give up. We're too close to our goal." My hands were bleeding, and I had bites all over my face, but I didn't care. I could rest later. Right now, I was too pumped up to stop. I was very tired and shed a lot of tears, but nothing or no one could get me to stop what I was doing.

Jonas came over to me and taking my hand said,

"Crystal, come sit down for a few minutes. Have some lemonade and eat something. If you don't, you won't have enough strength to finish. Matt is tired, too, and needs a little nourishment. Don't forget, he's only seven!"

"Okay, I guess I've gone a bit overboard, haven't I? Let's take a break for a while. I'm just so close to doing this I don't want to quit. We can work for another couple of hours, and then have to head to the house. Matt, let's take a break!"

Matt didn't have to be asked twice and came running over to the backpack that held our food and drink. "Let's eat!"

I was hungry but didn't want to take too much time away from my task at hand. I leaned back against a tree and looked at what we had done. I almost cried, because I hardly saw any progress. How many more days would we have to work on this? All I saw in front of me were more weeds and vines. We certainly would need more help, but where would it come from? Grandmother couldn't help, and Matt was so little, I couldn't expect him to work as hard as I was. Lost in my thoughts, I was surprised when Matt came running up to me. "Come on, lazy bones, let's get back to work!" He crossed his eyes at me and laughed.

That's all it took. I was revived and ready to go on. I figured if we could find one of the starting plants that seemed to be weaving all through the other weeds and chop it down, then maybe we would be able to pull away more of the thicket. I mean, it had only been there for fifty years. That shouldn't be so hard, should it? Oh, boy, I was really losing it.

Jonas had almost the same idea. He brought out the piece of rope and tied it to one of the trunks of a big vine. "Okay, let's all pull together on this one and see what happens. One – two – three – pull."

I was surprised and amazed to see how easily the vines and weeds pulled away from each other. "Jonas, you're wonderful!" The raven was jumping up and down on the cornerstone trunk. "I wish you could help us," was my response.

Persistence was finally paying off, and part of the outside of the pavilion came into view. If all of the weeds and vines were covering only the pavilion, then that could mean that the carousel should be in pretty good shape – right? We were doing a pretty good job for a couple of kids and an old man. I had to laugh at that thought. If only we had another person to help us, we could get finished faster. I might as well have asked for a tractor!

The raven continued to jump up and down, trying to get my attention. Surely, he didn't think he could help us, did he? I said, "My grandmother used to tell me about a young man who was changed into a raven. Can it be you?" and then, almost unconsciously, I said, "Cecil?"

169

There before my eyes, the raven was transformed into a young man in a cap. He stretched out his hands and looked at his fingers in amazement. He threw himself at my feet and cried, "Thank you, miss!"

Stunned at what had just happened, I yelled, "Matt and Jonas, come quickly! You're not going to believe this." Jonas and Matt came running to me where I held a huge vine and stood next to a young man who, up to a few seconds ago, had been a BIRD!

"Wow! Who is that, Crystal? Hi, I'm Mathew, but everyone calls me Matt. And this is Jonas. He's over a hundred years old. Looks pretty good, huh?"

I introduced Cecil to Matt and Jonas, and said, "Since we have all of that settled; I want to know all about you, and how you happened to turn up at the estate." We deserved a break from our work and finding out about Cecil was going to be very important, I thought. Then maybe he could help us with our big chore.

Twenty-Four
Cecil's Story

Cecil began his story. "My mother died when I was born. I was raised by the midwife who delivered me. She was one of those ladies in Savannah who could do all sorts of supernatural things, so I had a very interesting childhood." Cecil stopped for a minute and saw that we were listening to him and shaking our heads in disbelief. "She was good to me but also quite scary at times. I didn't feel like I was part of a real family, and that bothered me. I was determined to make a life for myself, and when I was fifteen, I left home for parts unknown. The midwife taught me a few 'tricks of the trade', as she called them. I learned how to turn things from their natural state into wood, but she said that I was never to take life from the living. Only dangerous animals should be turned into wood. It was not my right to do otherwise, or I would suffer the consequences. Then she disappeared. Of course, I discounted her warning. After all, I was fifteen and knew everything."

"Later that same year, I saw an ad in a newspaper calling for an experienced groomsman to

work at the Ashford Estate near Atlanta, taking care of a dozen or so expensive horses. Of course, I had no experience with horses, blue-blood or not, but figured I could infiltrate without too much difficulty. After all, I was empowered with certain abilities, wasn't I? It proved to be true, and I was hired by the chief trainer to take care of those magnificent creatures, especially a pure white one that was the daughter's personal horse."

Cecil paused for a minute, and I could see he was going to tell us something that was painful for him to recall. We all were silent and waited for him to continue.

"Things moved along very well for a while, until I decided I wasn't getting paid enough and began stealing – first, little pieces of silver from saddles, and then pieces from the main house. They trusted me, and I was, on occasion, invited in for refreshments. My small thefts went unnoticed I thought, but one day I was caught with my hand in the silver drawer by one of the downstairs maids. I was able to talk my way out of the indiscretion, returned the silver, and decided to back off for a while.

"A few months went by, and I was behaving well. In fact, my boss invited me to attend one of the big riding events as the private groom for the white horse. This pleased me, however, while polishing the gold and silver accessories for the saddle and bridle

172

to be worn by this magnificent steed, the temptation was more than I could stand, and I lifted the solid gold ring from the bridle and replaced it with a highly polished brass one. Little did I know I was being watched."

"The elder Mrs. Ashford made a practice of taking her daily walk from the main house to the stable to visit her precious Lady Starina, a twenty-five-year-old mare that she had ridden almost every day for decades. I didn't hear her approaching and wasn't aware that the old lady had seen my switch. The first that I knew she was around was when she told me I was to be fired as soon as her son returned that evening. I tried to talk my way out of this predicament, but it fell on deaf ears. Taking care to keep the gold ring on my person, I pondered what I was going to do about this mess. I decided that if I rode off on the white horse, I would be caught for sure and probably locked up for the duration of my life, or worse. Then I thought, why not use the magic and turn the rest of the horses into wooden ones, and then there wouldn't be any way I could be followed."

Matt couldn't stand it any longer, and said, "Bad move, Cecil." He was totally involved in the story.

Cecil shook his head and continued. "As I was carrying out my plan and had turned all but the white horse into wood, the midwife appeared again and reminded me that I was told not to take life from the

173

living. I never considered that included horses, just people. How narrow-sighted I was. I would suffer the consequences! No sooner had she uttered those words than she turned me into a big black raven. She cackled, 'The only way you can be turned human again is if a young girl, pure of spirit and good intentions, speaks your name. The only way that will happen is if you have the desire to help her and repent of your evil deeds.' Then she disappeared. Crystal, thank you for speaking my name."

"I am so happy I was able to do that for you. Your name just came out. My grandmother had told me part of your story when we first began this journey to help Crystal Ann. Please go on with your story."

"There I was, a raven, perched atop the stately white horse, flapping my wings and squawking loudly." He laughed at the mental picture, as did we. "So startled was the horse, that he fled in the direction of the woods with me on his back and the gold ring held tightly in my beak. When we finally stopped, I realized I was in a place I didn't recognize. The horse ran off, and there I was, confused, needless to say, and concerned as to what to do with the gold ring, I hid it in a hollow stump that turned out to be the cornerstone of the carousel building, until I could find a solution to my immediate problems. I wasn't sure I knew how to reverse this spell – that would happen only if my name was spoken, as I said before.

The chances of that happening, in my estimation, were about a million to one. It was at that moment that I pledged to repay whoever she was if I was ever lucky enough to find that special girl. I only knew I was in a lot more trouble than I had ever known."

Deafening silence followed Cecil's story. Matt cocked his head from side to side, trying to make sense of everything he had just heard. Jonas patted Cecil on the back. "I am sure glad you are a human now. You are a lot better looking than you were as a bird!"

"That's an amazing story, Cecil. I'm so glad you're here. Right now, we need to finish clearing away all of the weeds covering the building, so we can reach the carousel. Can you help us?" I touched my pendant and said a small, "Please?"

"I will be happy to do anything I can, if only you will tell me what your wishes are. Remember that I was locked in the body of a raven for over a hundred years. I have tried very hard to repent for what I had done. Matt, I apologize if I scared you. Crystal, thank you for not being afraid of me when you saw me after your parents' funeral. I just needed to get everyone's attention so I could help you and be free from the spell. I am very sure I will never do a dishonest thing again."

"What a way to learn a lesson," remarked Matt. "Let's get back to work before we all wake up and find *out that this has all been a dream."*

Thank goodness for this little guy and his sense of humor to lighten up the moment. For the next couple of hours, we tugged and cut and pulled at weeds until we had almost completely uncovered two sides of the pavilion. If we hadn't known who we were, we wouldn't have recognized us! Covered with mud and dirt from head to toe, we looked like mud statues instead of real people. I didn't care, though. It was worth all of the scrapes and cuts and bruises in order to finish my mission. I was determined that tomorrow would be the red-letter day we were all looking forward to.

The enclosure had doors that went all around the building. They were made of beautiful wood with glass inserts all the way to the top. Most of them were so dirty, we couldn't see inside, and a lot of them were broken. We didn't care, though; we were close to realizing our dream.

I turned to Cecil, my mind spinning. "None of what has happened in the last almost two weeks seems real, but here I am, standing with a young boy who used to be a raven offering to be my servant." Cecil laughed with me, because this was truly a fantasy, wasn't it?

It was getting time to head back to the house, and I turned to Cecil. "Would you like to come back to the house with us to meet Grandmother and have a little bite to eat? We'll show you all of the things we have assembled in order to solve the mystery."

"I would consider it an honor," Cecil said. "I know Jonas will keep things safe here until we return tomorrow."

Jonas tapped him on his arm. "You are in for a real treat, Cecil. Grandmother Bertie is a fabulous cook and will be very happy to meet you. I think you need to be back here before dark, however, and you may stay in my house that is located— "

Cecil interrupted him, "I know where the house is, Jonas. I have been all over every square inch of this property. I had nothing better to do all those years. And I know about the curfew but thank you for reminding me."

"I understand what you mean about having nothing better to do," laughed Jonas.

Matt and I hugged Jonas and told him we would see him the next day.

What a day! Matt, Cecil and I headed back to the house, and Cecil remarked about the clever way we had marked our path. "A couple of times, I had to scare off the young girl in the hat who was trying to remove the pieces of cloth. I think she finally gave up."

Matt jumped in and said he was sure glad about that, and added, "Thank you for taking care of that snake, Cecil. It was very brave of you."

"It was my pleasure, but I don't know if I could do that in my present state. As a raven, it wasn't a problem. I could do a lot of things then that I can't do since I am once again a human, but I surely don't ever want to go back to that form."

Whatever the next couple of days held for us, I was grateful for the time I had spent getting to know the people from the past. I would surely miss them.

Twenty-Five
Dinner Guest

We were close to the house when Matt turned to Cecil and told him that he thought the young girl, Daphne, had cast some kind of a spell on him a week or so before. He couldn't move for a while, and it was really scary. Looking him in the eye, he asked him to please let her know he didn't like it – if he ever saw her again. He ran off ahead of us, reaching the back porch first, already removing his shoes.

Cecil looked at me and I could tell he was nervous. "Don't worry about Grandmother," I assured him, "She is always ready to welcome my friends into her home and is the best grandmother ever! We need to wash up in the mudroom before going into the kitchen." As filthy as we were from all of the work, we should have used a hose to wash us all down.

Grandmother came into the mudroom, and was surprised by Cecil's appearance, but wasn't surprised that I had brought him there since I was sure Matt had already told her about him. She held out her hand. "Welcome to my home, Cecil, I am so happy to meet you."

He removed his cap, offered his hand, and then pulled back. "I would like to wash up first, Mrs. Le Grande, and then I'll shake your hand properly."

The table was set with colorful plates and bowls. Grandmother said food always tasted better if served on 'happy dishes'. I spied a pan of cornbread on the counter and a bowl of whipped butter and honey sitting next to it. Sweet potatoes were arranged on a plate, and her award-winning corn chowder with ham sat proudly in the center of the table in a large yellow tureen. There's nothing like comfort food.

"Auntie, are we going to have buttermilk?"

Matt's remark was a big, "Yuk! I tried it once and couldn't swallow it. Do I really have to drink it?"

Cecil remarked, "When I lived in Atlanta, one of my favorite meals included buttermilk. I agree that it is an acquired taste, but I love it."

That's all Matt needed to hear! He drank a second glass and decided he really liked it.

We finished Grandmother's wonderful dinner, and the four of us headed to the attic to go through everything Matt and I had found. When we entered the attic, I pointed to the trunks and the big cushion. I recounted, "I don't think you are a part of what we need to do to solve the mystery, but maybe a new set of eyes can show us something we have missed. The deadline is upon us, and I can't afford to make a

180

mistake. Everything has to work in the right order, and all I have are bits and pieces."

We spread everything out on the floor in front of us. Grandmother handed Matt the key that her mother had given her, and it opened the latch on the locked trunk.

We gathered around the trunk as Matt raised the lid. Inside the tray were stacks of notes and drawings and sketches of the six horses. They were the original drawings Michael had made for each of the horses. There were notes and samples of the wood he used and the sketches he made of White Magic. There also was a small child's school notebook.

A rolled-up piece of paper, when unfolded, outlined White Magic's champion-lineage. In addition, there were precise drawings for the carousel and dimensions and specifications for the calliope. Michael was more than just a wood carver, I thought. I urged Cecil to lift up the tray to see what was in the bottom of the trunk.

There were small carvings of each of the horses, measuring about eight inches tall and connected to a stand by a brass pole. Each bore an engraved plaque of its name. What a beautiful collection. Michael had probably planned to give them to Crystal Ann as part of her birthday present. I was pretty amazed at the collection and secretly wished to have it for my own. Heaving a big sigh, I said, "There isn't anything in

181

there to help with the mystery. Let's leave the notebook out, though. Maybe something in there will be interesting to read." Matt and Cecil scratched their heads. We were all visibly disappointed as we put the collection away.

The four of us studied the symbols on the incantation paper, each contributing our suggestions as to their meaning. Taking the series of words and putting them in a different order showed us we were no closer to understanding the outcome than we had been before.

"I hate to mention it," Cecil said, "but I have to leave. Jonas said I have to be back to his place before it gets dark. I don't want to stick around to find out the consequences. Thank you, Mrs. Le Grande, for your hospitality. I have had a wonderful time, and I'll see you all tomorrow."

Grandmother bade him goodnight, thanked him for coming and said that it had been a pleasure meeting him.

Matt and I walked Cecil downstairs. At the landing, I looked up and saw the stained-glass window. The flowers were back! I wondered if that meant that the carousel part of the mystery had been solved.

We reached the mudroom, and Cecil began to put on his boots. He really liked Matt's tennis shoes. "I have never seen any shoes like those." He was wearing boots, and they didn't look very comfortable. "I'll see you in the morning. Thanks for inviting me." He headed off in the direction of the woods. I knew he wasn't going to be able to stay around for much longer, and I was going to miss him and Jonas.

My thoughts were full of images and sounds and questions. As Matt and I walked back inside, we were both quiet. I knew that in a few days he would be returning to San Francisco, and Crystal Ann would be gone, as would Jonas and Cecil. Grandmother and I would be all alone again. The intensity of the past couple of weeks had filled up all of my waking (and sometimes sleeping) hours, and I was sure there was going to be a letdown. It made me very sad to think that my life was once again going to be predictable. The past events had helped to keep me moving in a positive direction, and for a little while, distracted my thoughts about life without my parents.

Twenty-Six
The Carousel

I arose very early the next morning, and as I tried to sit up, every muscle in my body refused to move like it was supposed to. I was sure I was not going to be able to get out of bed and into a nice hot shower. "Ouch! Oh, my goodness, what have I done? Okay, girl, this is an important day, and you can't be a sissy about this. Up you go!" I made one more big effort, and my feet finally hit the ground. I slowly moved toward the bathroom using the wall as support. I hurt in places I didn't know I had places, and with a lot of effort, I was in the bathroom and able to turn on the shower. I slowly stepped into the healing water and wondered how Matt was doing.

After standing in the shower for a few minutes, my muscles began to feel a lot better. I stretched my arms and legs, and soon I was ready to get back to the task at hand.

Once in the hall, Matt approached me walking very slowly toward me. "Hi, cuz, how are you feeling? I hurt all over."

"I am sore, too, but feel better after my shower.

There is nothing that will keep me from finishing this mission. We are so close, and I'm excited. How about you?"

"Oh, I'll be just fine once I get moving. We'll work twice as hard today. Are you as excited as I am?"

"You betcha, Cuz! Let's get going." We headed down the eight steps to the landing. The carousel horse once again appeared in the stained-glass window.

"I'm hungry. We are going to need a lot of nourishment today. I can't wait to see Jonas and Cecil again."

"Me, too."

As we walked into the kitchen, Grandmother turned and gave us a big smile. "How are my two favorite detectives today? Hungry? Sore? I hope you put something on all of those scrapes."

"Yes, we did, and boy are we hungry and sore. We are so excited about today. The pavilion is so big, we didn't know whether we could uncover it or not, but with all of us pulling and tugging and cutting, we are beating the weeds. We're determined that they are not going to beat us! My tummy is doing flip flops. Let's eat fast and get out of here, Matt."

"You betcha, boss."

She reminded us that we should take a rest now and then and be sure to drink lots of water. It was *going to be a very hot and humid day, and she didn't want us to get sick. We assured her we would, and after giving her a kiss, Matt took the lunch and thermos full of water and put them in his backpack.*

One more big hug, and Matt and I headed for our shoes. We checked inside each shoe for critters and smiled quietly at each other when nothing dropped out. He had learned so much in the past couple of weeks, and in no time at all, he would be leaving. That made me sad.

"Okay, let's go!" And he ran out the door with me behind him.

I found myself skipping along humming a tune I had never heard before, but I was so happy, I thought I was going to explode. Matt also skipped along and touched the pieces of cloth as we headed toward our ultimate goal. Off in the distance, I heard music and knew we were getting closer.

The scent of gardenias filled the air around where we walked, and I turned to see Daphne, raising her fists in the air in defiance. "You are never going to stop us, Daphne. Go back where you came from or make up your mind to stop being so angry. We can be friends, but not unless you stop all of this bad stuff." Daphne faded away, and I continued along the path toward my goal.

In the distance, we saw Jonas and Cecil hard at work pulling weeds away from our treasure. They turned toward us and Matt started running. "Hey! Here we are!"

I found myself running as well, and when I neared the building, I could see that they had cleared more weeds away. "Hi, y'all. You have done so much work. Thank you. Okay, we're ready to work." Pulling on some heavy gloves, I joined Cecil who yanked at a big vine that wouldn't release its decades-long hold on the building. It took us about five minutes of hard pulling, but we finally won. When it sprung loose, we fell backwards and landed on the ground laughing. We repeated that routine for hours until finally the last bits of weeds and vines were reduced to a pile of debris.

Matt, Jonas, Cecil, and I stepped back and stared at the pavilion in front of us. I began to cry, mostly because we had succeeded in finding the carousel. Matt put his arms around me and in his very special way said, "Hey, boss, we did it! Are we a good team, or what?" I had to laugh and definitely felt better.

"Matt, you said a mouthful. Okay, let's get these doors open and find our grand prize!"

Jonas went from door panel to panel, and with a lot of heaving and with help from Cecil eventually moved one piece at a time and folded them back like an accordion. Some of the glass was broken, and he was very careful not to cut himself, and warned us to watch where we were walking.

187

It took quite a while to open up all of the doors, and when they had all been moved away, what we saw was something I never could have imagined. It was like finding a huge diamond. "Oh, my goodness! How beautiful! I can't breathe!"

Matt ran over to me and patted me on the back. "Are you going to be all right?" I said I thought so, but I needed a minute to catch my breath.

The carousel Crystal Ann's father had created slowly turned in the middle of the pavilion. Mounted on a platform of about twenty feet in diameter were six full-sized horses, each with a brass pole inserted through its back. Attached to the platform was a beautiful canopy supported by more brass poles. Multi-colored mirrors decorated its top, and the horses were gliding up and down as the carousel turned. Each of the six horses was adorned with different colorful bridles and saddles. The reins were made of leather. I was awestruck!

Matt looked over at me as I stepped up on the platform. He jumped on without being asked and looked like someone had just given him a stack of Dick Tracy comics.

My heart pounded, and my knees shook. Directing my question to Jonas, "Can you please stop the carousel from moving for a few minutes, so we can take a good look at all of the horses?"

"Indeed, Miss Crystal." He entered a little room

located in the middle, and it began to slow down. The music had slowed down as well.

"Jonas," I asked, when he stepped back onto the platform, "Who else could have been inside the pavilion keeping the calliope working all of these years?"

"It was my father. He loved this as much as we all did and made a vow that he would keep the music playing in order to bring peace to the spirits. He is gone now, because his job is finished."

There was no reason for me not to believe what he had said was true, and with misty eyes, I began to explore the horses, stopping at each one. I rubbed their beautiful bodies with my hands and whispered that I thought they were the most special creatures in the world. I remembered reading that Michael had modeled them after famous horses and painted the saddles and bridles they wore exactly like the original ones. The reins were made from leather, and even though they were very old, were still soft. There was a lot I didn't understand about all of this, standing there next to those beautiful works of art.

I jumped off the platform and picked up the stack of cleaning rags I had brought along so I could wipe off each of the horses. It was important that each of them looked their best in time for Crystal Ann and Michael to reunite.

Matt was with Jonas in the center of the

carousel, inspecting the calliope that had made all of that wonderful music. I walked around to each of the horses and brushed off bits of spider webs and imagined the care that Michael had taken carving and sanding and gently oiling the wood to keep it from cracking. I carefully wiped down each horse, taking care to talk to each one, letting it know it was loved. I moved on, all the while wondering if the next horse would be the replica of White Magic. There was a metal engraved plate on the bridle of each horse, showing its name. I polished it as best I could, talking to it as if it were real. The next horse was black with a white mane and tail. I patted it, admiring its beautiful legs bent in mid-stride. He looked like he was galloping. I thought I was doing a good job and felt a presence standing behind me. As I turned, Michael stood there with a big smile on his face. Then he faded away.

The label on the next horse in line was White Magic. I was so excited, I could hardly stand it. I touched his nose, admiring how lifelike he was. He was completely white with a white mane and tail. His only color was a small black diamond on his face. I once again felt the presence of Crystal Ann and was determined to complete my mission. I put my arms around his neck and told him I was going to see that he would always be loved and taken care of. I rubbed his highly polished paint with a smooth, soft cloth and polished his nameplate with the care of a jeweler. My heart was so full, I didn't know whether to laugh or cry. All of our hard work had paid off, and we were going to be able to complete our mission in time for Crystal Ann to be reunited with her father. I felt so good. Matt, Jonas, and Cecil walked toward me, and we all hugged.

"Thank you so much for all of your help. I've completed my mission now, as I promised I would. Let's tell Grandmother. We'll be able to come back tomorrow and finish what we started two weeks ago."

Jonas and Cecil waved to us as Matt and I headed back to the house, two very tired but happy kids.

Twenty-Seven
Chloe's Thoughts

Chloe's parents had sent her to her Grandma Crystal's house to get to know her better. She and her family had just moved back to the Atlanta area after living in another part of the country from the time she was three. She hadn't been able to come for an extended visit until this summer, and the only times she had seen her grandma was on holidays at her house, but she never really got to know her.

Chloe thought that coming to this old house was like a jail sentence. What in the world did she have in common with this old woman? She was nice enough, she guessed, but didn't her parents know that the summer vacation was so she could have fun with her friends?

It had rained the whole time she was there. It was too quiet out there in the country, and the big, old house was like a barn to her. The floors creaked, and nothing was modern. The whole experience seemed like something from an old *Twilight Zone* episode. She couldn't talk on her cell phone because the signal didn't stay strong long enough to even get the latest news from her friends. She was missing the biggest party of the year. The boy she really, really liked was going to be there and if she didn't show up, he would surely forget all about her! Life as she knew it was over!

That's why she stole the keys and went into the attic. She thought that at least she might find something interesting there. How stupid was she to leave the keys on the outside of the door and get locked in? The rain pounded the windows so loudly that she couldn't hear herself think, much less have her grandma hear her call for help.

Finding the journal began to make a change in Chloe's thinking and in her life. At first, she thought the writings were lame, but as she continued to read the journal, she moved from disbelief to reality to disbelief again. This had to be fiction!

She didn't really know anything about her grandma. No one seemed to talk about family very much at home, and she didn't know why, but she was definitely going to find out – if she ever got out of that attic.

What a terrible thing it would be to lose her parents like her grandma had at the very same age she was. Chloe knew that she hated some of the restrictions her folks set, and maybe she didn't totally understand why, but she would make a promise to do better and follow the rules.

She had never had the kind of responsibility given to her that her grandma had when, as a girl of twelve, she learned that she was the only one who could help a young girl reunite with her father. A dead girl, no less! Chloe used to gripe when her mother asked her to put the dishes into the dishwasher and be sure her clothes were picked up. Never again. She was going to try her best to make things easier for her mom and dad. Being an only child, she realized how many privileges she had and how she had taken advantage of them.

Crystal Ann had been the center of her father's world, and she never even knew her mother. Chloe couldn't imagine not having her mom around. She had read about the wonderful pieces of history packed away in trunks in the attic. She now looked at the three mannequins in front of her and was able to appreciate the work that had gone into those beautiful gowns. She still wished they would appear to her as they had to her grandma, and to smile at her – but they still had no faces. Her grandma had been able to speak with her grandmother because she believed she could. Mysterious writings, words, a carousel, a gold ring, Crystal Ann and her father, a raven that became a boy, an old slave and a crazy girl in a floppy hat – these were the things that her grandma had to contend with while trying to do the right thing and help someone she didn't even know; except that she had been named for her.

This was just too much to swallow. She needed to find out more, since it looked like she was probably going to be in the attic for a long time. She was amazed at everything she had read and seen. As she looked around the attic, she realized how much trouble she was going to be in once her grandma found her – if she found her. She was beginning to understand how much family meant to her, and right then, all she wanted to do was see her grandma and ask her to forgive her. Of course, a good meal would fit into her plans nicely. However, she was locked in, and no one knew where she was.

Chloe sat down and fell back into the journal.

Twenty-Eight
The Final Clue

*Grandmother was still in the attic when Matt and I
ran upstairs, eager to tell her we had uncovered the
carousel. We didn't want to startle her. Sitting there,
she looked a lot like her mother surrounded by all her
family things. She was studying the paper and had not
heard us enter the room. We stood at the doorway
and listened to her.*

*"Mother, can you please appear one more time
to help us with this? I want to be of some help to
Crystal and know there is an order to the way things
are supposed to go, but I just can't make it out."*

*We stayed in the shadows so as not to interrupt
her, or the visions that might appear. I silently asked
my great-grandmother to come back again. I firmly
believe that GG heard my plea, and in a moment, her
slow, Southern drawl came through to Grandmother
very clearly.*

*"Study the paper and all of the symbols. Notice
the unusual way it was folded. Fold the paper back
as it had been. If you have gathered everything, the
symbols should form one complete picture. The*

actual incantation is sealed with wax, and once the symbols are reunited, the incantation may be read, thus bringing things back to where they need to be. Remember, that the only person who can say the incantation is Crystal, as that is the request from Crystal Ann."

"Mother," Grandmother began, "why can't I see you this time? I can only hear your voice. I miss you ever so much."

"It is not time for me to reappear, dear Bertha. You have all of the ingredients now to make this request a reality. I think that Crystal and Mathew have done a wonderful job in continuing to search for clues. It is a very loving and unselfish thing they have done. And now, I must leave you. Perhaps I will see you again before too long." With those words, her voice trailed off, and all was silent.

"Thank you for all of your assistance, Mother, and thank you for the key. Seeing all of the sketches and small-scale carousel horses was a big surprise and very special to all of us."

Matt and I didn't want to interfere with her moment. We were a day away from the deadline, and I didn't know if we could have finished everything in time otherwise. Matt and I cleared our throats as we entered the room. "Grandmother," I said, "we uncovered the carousel all the way, and it's the most beautiful thing I have ever seen. All the horses are in *perfect condition, and the calliope is running, too. I can't believe this is all happening."*

"I am so happy you finished that part of the mystery, Crystal. Things are really heading in the right direction."

Matt and I sat down on the floor in front of her. "We overheard everything Great-Grandmother said to you. I think now is the time to open the sealed incantation," I said.

She was about to hand me the sealed incantation when she was interrupted by her mother's voice again. "Bertha, the incantation cannot be opened until immediately before the exact moment it is to be read. Keep it close to you until tomorrow evening, which would have been Crystal Ann's twelfth birthday. Cecil will tell Crystal when it is time to read it. Certain other things need to happen before the process can be completed, and all will be revealed."

Matt and I were happy to hear my great-grandmother's voice, and I glanced over to Grandmother, in time to see her wipe tears from her eyes with a lace handkerchief she always carried. I know how much she loved her mother, and emotions were very strong in that room right then. I missed my mom so much, and I felt a big lump in my throat. I wished I could hear her voice one more time.

"Mother," Grandmother said, "thank you for coming back. I have needed your guidance in this

trying time. We all are experiencing many different emotions right now. I know everything will be fine, and we will do as you say. I love you very much."

"I am so proud of all of you, especially you, Crystal. It is difficult for someone so young to understand how important it is to put someone else's needs over his or her own. Your parents will be very proud of you, and your good deeds will not go unrewarded. I have to leave you now, knowing you will be fine in every way." With those words, my GG's voice fell silent.

We sat very still for a long time. In the distance, the wind caused the leaves to sway in tempo with the music. It was what you might call surreal. I held on to my crystal horse and reached out to Grandmother and Matt. We held hands and listened to the wind and the music, knowing that tomorrow night this adventure would be over. It was sad but knowing Crystal Ann and her father would have the opportunity to reunite put a smile in my heart. I felt very grown up all of a sudden, not really sure I liked the feeling.

Grandmother stood, "Would you like some hot chocolate with tiny marshmallows? I think I have some peanut butter cookies to go with it."

"Me?" Matt's reply was predictable. "I'm always up for dessert. Crystal, are you going to join us?"

"I think I'll stay in the attic for a little longer to

go over everything I am supposed to do tomorrow night, but I won't stay up here too long." I was beginning to feel very comfortable there. Grandmother kissed me on the forehead and Matt gave me the thumbs-up sign, as they walked out of the room.

Something prompted me to look in the box that held Crystal Ann's keepsakes. I don't know why, but I thought that holding onto her locket might bring her back to talk to me one last time. I gently opened the lid of the jewelry box, and the calliope music in the distance became louder than I had ever heard it before. It startled me, and I quickly closed it. What was that all about? Was I not supposed to disturb anything again? The music stopped and so did the wind. I quickly looked around the room and headed for the door. I vowed it would be a long time before I would come up here again, unless, of course, there was more to find out about our interesting family.

I walked to the landing and stopped again. The flowers stared back at me. Continuing down the next eight steps, a real feeling of sadness overcame me. This adventure would soon be over. Matt would return to San Francisco, and I would soon be back in school. Boring! But right now, the thought and smells of peanut butter cookies and hot chocolate beckoned me.

Grandmother sat on a stool stirring her hot

200

chocolate. There was a glow about her face. The circumstances surrounding the Crystal Ann situation had allowed her to carry on a special conversation with her mother. Matt was standing in front of the counter, first on one foot and then the other, chomping on a cookie. He looked very mature to me, older than his seven years.

This little boy who used to bug me had become a capable, fun, clever young man. I was going to miss him very much. I hoped that someday I would be able to fly on a plane by myself and visit him.

I didn't think my adventure would have been as successful without his help. By the look on his face, I could tell he was thinking about all that had happened in the past couple of weeks. I had to laugh silently, picturing him telling his friends about his journey into the past. I hoped they wouldn't make fun of him. In my eyes, he was my hero.

I poured a cup and topped it with three marshmallows, one pink, one green, and one white. Grandmother always had colored marshmallows for our hot chocolate. She said eating should be fun! Armed with two cookies, I joined Matt at the counter.

"We are a pretty good team, Sherlock."

"The best," Matt answered.

Twenty-Nine
Real White Magic

I awoke early the next morning and lay in my bed, listening to the rustle of the wind through the trees. It should be a beautiful day, even though I had not forgotten what I had to do that evening. As I recalled the events of the past two weeks and again heard my GG's voice, and saw the pride in my grandmother's eyes, I knew there was nothing to do except what was expected of me.

I slowly sat up on the edge of the bed as I looked at my clock on the nightstand. It was only 7:00 a.m.! I listened to see if I could hear Matt stirring, and the only sound I heard was the tick-tock of the big grandfather clock that had been in the family for generations, and as predictable as ever, it struck seven times. Surely that would awaken Matt and Grandmother. I listened but didn't hear anything.

Maybe I'd just lie back down for a few minutes and go over everything I was supposed to do. However, instead, I fell asleep to the sound of the calliope music and the wind.

Matt was shaking my shoulders, trying to wake

me up. "Crystal, it is almost nine o'clock."

"Nine o'clock?" I screamed at him. "Why did you let me sleep so late? I know it isn't your fault, but I am disappointed I've let half of the morning go by already. I have so much to do and want to clean up the rest of the horses."

Matt said, "It isn't my fault you slept so late and besides, it isn't that late. I figured you must have needed the rest."

"It's just that it is such a big day, and I don't want to waste any of it. Will you please forgive me?"

"Sure, what are cousins for?" I threw a pillow at him as he ran out the door.

I followed the yummy smells into the kitchen. Freshly-squeezed orange juice was in a glass pitcher and little link sausages were sizzling in a pan on the stove. That's what I needed – a hearty breakfast to help me through the day.

Grandmother asked as I entered the kitchen, "Are blueberry crepes okay with you?" She also had made up some fried chicken for us to take with us for lunch. She was a pretty amazing grandmother.

"Oh, boy," said Matt. "I love blueberry crepes – they sound French – and fried chicken." I don't think he had ever had crepes, but he'd eat anything!

"I'll come to the carousel later in the afternoon, so you can complete your project. And you'll have time to read the incantation in time." Grandmother *sounded very sure we were almost at the end of our mystery.*

Matt told her that he thought someone should come back and walk down there with her. "A lady should always be accompanied by a gentleman on such a journey."

She and I almost split our sides, joining in his enthusiasm, wondering where he had heard that. I apologized. "I didn't mean to laugh, but you looked so serious."

"I am serious. One of us 'men' will come back and fetch Aunt Bertie, and there will be no arguments. Okay?"

"Thank you, kind sir," said Grandmother. "Far be it for me to argue with something that makes that much sense. I do appreciate it. I shall be ready for my escort and thank you for thinking of me." She messed up his hair and kissed him on the cheek.

After my hearty breakfast, I felt I was ready to face that important day. I had a pail with soapy water and several rags and towels. Even though the horses looked like they had been taken care of pretty well, I still wanted to do a final cleaning on each of them. Grandmother handed me a broom to sweep the platform. Matt grabbed the basket with the fried chicken and off we went to meet up with Jonas and Cecil. I had a knot in the pit of my stomach the size of a baseball and was having a hard time thinking about everything I was supposed to do. Oh well, Grandmother and Cecil would help me.

Fortunately, the pieces of cloth were still tied to the bushes, and as we approached the carousel, Jonas and Cecil greeted us. Matt ran toward the two men and jumped into Jonas's arms. Cecil took the pail and rags and offered me his hand.

Cecil told me to come with him and we would finish cleaning the horses. Jonas had worked all night on the calliope and had it shiny as new. I felt that Cecil, in his own way, was as sad as I was to see the end to that day.

None of what had occurred in the last two weeks seemed real, but there I was, standing on a carousel with a young boy who used to be a raven and had offered to be my servant.

Cecil had previously asked me what my wishes were since I had spoken his name. He wanted to repay me for the deed that allowed him once again to become a human boy. Suddenly, I knew the answer. "Cecil, do you think you could turn a wooden horse into a real one?"

He replied, "I am fairly certain I can. Why?"

"All of my life, I have wanted a real horse like White Magic to ride."

I gently rubbed his wooden body, paying special attention to his face and lovingly spoke to him about how wonderful it would be for him to be with Crystal

Ann. I didn't know if he knew he had been specially made by her father as a token of his love, so I told him the story.

The four of us worked for several hours sweeping and washing and polishing everything. Jonas had done a beautiful job on the calliope, so he pitched in and helped us. The next thing we knew, it was close to sundown, and as I looked in the direction of the house, I saw Grandmother coming down the path escorted by Jonas. I hadn't seen him leave, because I was busy with the horses. I jumped off the platform and ran to them.

I was so excited and took Grandmother by the hand to show her the beautiful merry-go-round. Jonas helped her up onto the platform. We walked from horse to horse as she read the little plaques on each one. Saving the best for last, I stopped. "Grandmother, I want you to meet White Magic, the most beautiful horse in the world."

"It is such a pleasure to meet you, White Magic. You are, indeed, a beautiful steed."

"How about if we all take a little spin now that we have finished our cleaning up of the horses?" Jonas asked.

"You bet," said Matt, as he jumped up and ran to a big black horse.

"Grandmother, let me help you." As much as I had wanted to ride White Magic, I wanted her to have *the privilege at that moment.*

Cecil and I each chose a horse and gave the high sign to Jonas who stood in the center of the carousel, his hand poised above the handle that would start our ride. He pushed the handle and jumped onto one of the remaining horses. We took those moments to laugh once again, after all of the drama and sadness, death and spells and uncertainty. Michael's creation was finally being enjoyed. I looked in the direction of the back of the property and saw an angry Daphne with her hands on her hips. A shiver ran through my body, but I was determined not to let her get to me.

After the ride ended, I climbed onto White Magic's back and finding the courage, asked, "Cecil, please cast your spell so I can ride him." Cecil agreed, but Jonas expressed his worries about White Magic being too hard to ride. "It will be too dangerous."

I said, "I have taken riding lessons for years and will be very careful." Looking at my grandmother, I pleaded with her to let me do it.

Grandmother reluctantly agreed. "Be aware that it is almost sunset, and you can't be late, or you know the consequences. Please be careful."

Cecil uttered a few simple words. White Magic was transformed into a beautiful white horse and pawed anxiously at the platform to stretch his legs.

"Oh, my gosh," I gasped. "He is real, and ready

to go. Hey, Matt, want to come along with me?"

Matt was obviously scared, and said, "No, you go ahead. Have a good time."

I took up the reins and White Magic leapt off the carousel. I said a silent prayer that we would be safe. I was so ecstatic – a horse of my own, finally! Deep down, I knew I couldn't keep him, but I was going to savor that moment. Together we galloped across the fields of the estate.

Brought back to reality instantly, Chloe flipped through the pages of the journal, but frustration set in. She couldn't find any more entries. What happened? This wasn't fair. She needed to know what happened after she rode away on the horse!

She looked around for more journals and found the small school notebook and began to look through it, perhaps to find some more answers. OMG, the candle just burned out, and there wasn't another one, and she was in the dark! "Grandma, where are you?" She started to cry, feeling scared and very much alone.

Thirty
The Search

Crystal was downstairs and entered from outside with a flashlight. She met Matt in the entry coming up from the basement. Matt had been living in the house with Crystal for many years since his wife died. Crystal's husband had died several years before. They had become very close over the fifty years since their adventure and were a great comfort to each other and both loved the old house.

"Did you find her?" Crystal asked, as Matt joined her. "I shouldn't have been so hard on her. I understand how she felt, but I still want her to be here with me for a couple of weeks. I thought she'd enjoy it. We have spent so little time together, and since they moved to Atlanta from California, I thought I'd be able to see her more often and really get to know her." Crystal was beside herself with worry.

"Well, you were kind of a goody-goody, you know. Maybe you came on too strong. She is at a very impressionable age – not a kid, yet not quite an adult. Don't you remember being that age?" Matt hadn't changed very much in his attitude about things.

"Of course, I do, that's why I am so worried about her."

"Have you tried the attic?"

"I forbade her to go up there, and besides, it was locked." Then she remembered seeing the drawer half open and headed for the stairs.

Matt followed behind her as close as he could and rolled his eyes just like he used to do when they were kids.

Climbing the stairs to the second floor, Crystal had to stop at the top to catch her breath. She remembered when she could take the steps two at a time. Slowly, she began to climb the stairs. As she approached the door, she saw the key sticking out of the lock. She turned the knob and opened the door to enter the dark room. Chloe burst into her arms, nearly knocking her down.

"Grandma, I'm so sorry. I took the keys and got locked in. I found some candles, but they burned down. I'm scared of the dark. Please forgive me. I didn't mean to worry you."

Crystal gave Chloe a big hug and said it was all right, just as long as she was okay. "I'm sorry I was so hard on you, honey. I seem to have forgotten what it was like to be your age."

"Hey, are we ever going to eat?" Matt entered the attic, exhausted from the climb. "How're you doing, Chloe? Are you hungry?"

"Uncle Matt! I'm starving. Grandma, do you still have that chicken cordon bleu? I can't wait to dig into it."

This wasn't exactly the way Crystal had planned for their first dinner to be, but it would be just fine. There must be a way to get closer to Chloe and have the remainder of their time together more pleasant.

Chloe entered the dining room and took her place at the table. Matt said a short blessing, and he and Chloe dug in with a vengeance.

With her mouth full, Chloe said, "It's so good. I had no idea chicken could taste so wonderful. And there is cheese and ham in it. Wow! I read that expression in your journal. I think Uncle Matt used it a lot."

Matt lowered his head and pretended to be embarrassed. Then he chuckled.

"Slow down, honey. I know you were hungry, but you could get a stomach ache if you eat too fast."

As he began to say something, Crystal stopped him. "Matt, don't talk with your mouth full."

Matt burped, and he and Chloe giggled at her grandma, who was looking aghast and stern.

Chloe finished and launched into her questions. "Grandma, was the story I read in your journal real? Was Cecil really a raven? What happened to Jonas? Did Crystal Ann unite with her dad? Why did you stop writing in the journal?"

Matt and Crystal looked across the table at one another in silence.

"Uncle Matt, you were there, what happened? You were having a great time, playing detective and all that. I bet you had a really great time, especially riding on the carousel."

"Crystal is the one to tell you the rest of the story, Chloe."

Crystal nodded, realizing she would be telling the end of the story for the first time. "Chloe, go get ready for bed. I'll be up to tuck you in."

"And you'll tell me the rest?" Crystal nodded.

Thirty-One
The Whole Story

Crystal slowly climbed the stairs to the second floor
and entered Chloe's room that had been her room
when she lived with her Grandmother Bertie.
Memories came flooding back like a river. Those
were happy days until the end, and she hoped that she
could set things right with Chloe, so they could
develop a good relationship.

A glass case displaying the six carvings of the
carousel horses that had been packed away for so
many years hung above the dresser. Several small
miniatures painted by Crystal's mother lovingly sat
on top of the dresser on little easels next to the jewelry
box that had belonged to Crystal Ann. It had been
Bertie's decision to place these treasures where they
could be appreciated.

Chloe hopped into bed as soon as her grandma
entered. "Please start with 'Once Upon a Time'."

"I can't, honey. This is not a happy tale." She
took a deep and recapped: "You've read about
Crystal Ann and Michael, Cecil, and Jonas."

And Chloe added, "And White Magic."

Crystal continued, "He was so beautiful. I had always wanted a horse just like him. That day, I rode him for the first and last time. It was like we were one. We rode like the wind. It seemed we were meant to be together. I knew I had to get back before sunset. I only had a few minutes, but I couldn't let him go. Just a little longer, just a few minutes more. I was so happy; why should I have to give him up for a girl who had died a long time ago? Of course, I was wrong and selfish. Daphne stepped out of the woods and startled me. She said that I was just the same as she was, a poor girl with no parents; unloved, wanting something I could never have. I told her that I may have been an orphan, but I was not hateful and angry like her, and besides I was loved by my grandmother and my cousin. Daphne was angrier than I had ever imagined, and she banged two sticks together and spooked White Magic. He bolted, and I was thrown off. He galloped off and disappeared.

"I guess I was unconscious, but in a few minutes, I woke up. Daphne laughed and told me it was too late for me to help Crystal Ann. She had won again. I didn't know what she meant by that, but all I knew was that I needed to find everyone who had been counting on me. It was a disaster, to say the least."

Grandma was quiet for a few minutes and then continued. "By the time I finally returned, Cecil had

214

turned back into a raven, because he was unable to help Crystal Ann and Michael be together. Matt and Jonas were disappointed and Grandmother was, well, that was the worst. I had let her down. It would be two generations before Crystal Ann could try again to be with her father. I had ruined everything. That is why I didn't finish the story. When I reached the end, it was too painful to remember."

Comforting her, Chloe said, "I know that was very hard for you to remember. I'm so sorry, but you tried."

"Not hard enough," was her reply. Crystal reached over to brush back her hair from her face and gently ran her fingers down her check. Chloe closed her eyes and gave a big sigh. She remembered reading about Bertie's touch and how important it was to Crystal. In that moment, a bond formed between them that would always remain.

"I apologize for not being more fun and being so hard on you. I was just trying to keep from making mistakes but was probably making more. I knew you were missing your friends."

"There is a big party in Atlanta at a friend's home. All of my friends will be there, and there is this guy I really like. He is really hot and very smart, and he likes me. It just seemed like this was the wrong time to visit, under the circumstances."

Crystal got an idea. "Why don't I drive you to

Atlanta so you can go to that party? Would you like that? And by the way, will it be chaperoned?"

Making a face almost like the rolling the eyes thing, Chloe said, "Oh, Grandma, would you do that for me? Maybe Uncle Matt could come with us so you will have company. You two could go to the movies or something, and then come and pick me up. And yes, the parents will be there."

Crystal kissed her goodnight and before she left the room, Chloe asked, "Grandma, could I help Crystal Ann?"

"I don't know if it is possible, honey."

"I remember that Crystal Ann said she would have to wait two more generations. I'm in the right generation. Maybe Great-Grandmother Bertie can help, the way that Great-Great-Grandmother Eunice did before."

"I didn't think kids nowadays believed this kind of stuff." She choked up a bit deep in her heart.

Chloe made it easy. "Tomorrow morning, we'll go up to the attic and talk to GG."

Crystal kissed her forehead and rose to leave. At the doorway, she turned and said, "Thank you."

Chloe blew her a kiss.

*****

The next morning, Crystal and Chloe climbed the

stairs. The stained-glass window was a horse again. They noticed it, drew in their breath, and smiled. It was more than a good sign; it was a cosmic sign.

Crystal approached a trunk that moved across the floor toward them. It was deja vu.

Chloe jumped back and laughed. "I read about that happening, but never thought I would experience it myself. I wouldn't have missed this for anything."

Crystal smiled as she opened the trunk. She felt a presence and turned to find Matt standing in the doorway.

"I didn't want to miss this."

"Uncle Matt, come help us." Chloe was so excited she could hardly speak.

Chloe spread out the paper and the sealed incantation. "Okay, Grandma, call for your Grandmother Bertie.

Crystal took a deep breath and did nothing. "Come on, you can do it."

"Grandmother, please come to me and help me. I am so sorry I disappointed you and everyone so long ago and want to make it right."

It seemed like years before Bertie appeared, but there she was, looking just like Crystal had described her in the journal. Chloe almost fell against the wall. No one would ever believe her.

"I already forgave you, my darling Crystal. We have all done things in our past that we are ashamed

217

of. You were always the light of my life and taking care of you was the greatest honor. I understood why you did what you did, and you couldn't have imagined that Daphne would try to hurt you."

"Oh, Grandmother, thank you for understanding. I never could have been able to get through these years unless I knew in my heart that you had forgiven me."

"Crystal dear, remember that it is important to make things right. The ceremony is exactly the same, except that Chloe must speak the words."

Crystal reached out wanting to make a connection with her grandmother, but knew it was impossible. Memories of her childhood came flooding back at that moment, and she silently wished she could relive those times when she and her grandmother were so close. "I love you so much. Thank you for taking part in helping Chloe finish what I was unable to do."

Bertie was touched by the beautiful words spoken by her granddaughter. She needed to continue before the tears and the lump in her throat wouldn't permit her to do so. "By the way, give Chloe the crystal horse to wear around her neck. It should belong to her now. Crystal Ann will be waiting. Goodbye."

Bertie faded away.

Crystal moved next to Chloe and removed the necklace from around her neck. "As you know, this has been very special to me. I can't think of anyone I would rather have wear it than you. Take good care of it and you will find it a great source of comfort in times of need."

The sniffing sound made Crystal and Chloe turn just in time to see Matt wipe his eyes with his shirttail. They continued speaking, not wanting to embarrass him.

"Tonight, we will go to the carousel before sunset, armed with the parts of the puzzle to make things right for Crystal Ann and Michael and White Magic."

"Do you think Cecil and Jonas will be there?" Chloe thought it was a logical question.

"I don't know, honey, but we will find out, I'm sure."

*****

Chloe had the small notebook on her nightstand, and she picked it up and began moving through the pages. It was Daphne's notes about her relationship with Crystal. Her poor handwriting could still be read. Chloe was heartsick as she read:

I made a friend today. Her name is Crystal Ann. She is a very nice girl. She lives in a big house with her father. Her mother died when she was just a baby. They have a lot of money, I think. Their house is beautiful, and I am happy I can spend time there.

Crystal Ann got a big white horse for her birthday. She doesn't spend very much time with me now, because she is riding all of the time, and winning ribbons and trophies in horse shows. It's almost like she doesn't know I exist.

Maybe if White Magic ran away, Crystal Ann would have more time for me. How can I make that happen? I know where she rides every day. I can scare the horse and when she falls off, I can run in a save her, then she will like me again.

Today was the day I waited for Crystal Ann and White Magic at the wall she likes to jump. I had two big sticks and when they came close to the wall, I banged them together, scaring White Magic. He stopped very fast, and Crystal Ann couldn't hold on and flew over his head, hitting her head on the wall. The horse ran off. I ran over to her and she looked like she was knocked out and I got very scared, and thought she was hurt very bad.

I heard today that Crystal Ann died when she fell off the horse and hit her head on the wall. It is all my fault. I didn't want anything to happen to her; I just wanted my friend back. White Magic came back to the stables, and Mr. Le Grande doesn't even want to look at him. He thinks it was the horse's fault that she is dead. I need to tell him it was because of me. He had been like a father to me when Crystal Ann was alive. I'll try to spend some more time with him and try to

220

tell him the truth. I am so sorry it happened. Maybe I can be a substitute daughter to him. That might help him feel better.

I hang around watching Mr. Le Grande work, asking all sorts of questions. He doesn't talk very much, but I don't think he minds if I am there. I am very lonesome and miss Crystal Ann. I'll go over there tomorrow to explain what happened to her.

Today I asked Mr. Le Grande if I could ride White Magic and he was very angry and told me to go away. Doesn't he think I am good enough to ride his daughter's horse? I was very sad and thought he would like me to be a new daughter to him, but no one will ever be good enough to take her place.

Maybe I am only an orphan, but that is not a reason why I should be ignored by someone I thought was my friend. I swear I will make him suffer now. Who does he think he is, with all of his wealth and everything? I guess I am just not good enough for him anymore. I'll ride White Magic anyway and that will show him!

Thirty-Two
The Moment of Truth

Crystal hadn't been out to the carousel since that awful day, so she didn't know what it would be like, or if Cecil was still a raven, and whether Jonas was still hanging around. It was close to seven the next evening and the trio, armed with their special treasures, headed to the back of the property as Matt and Crystal had done so many years before.

As they walked along, Matt said, "I had ventured back there on a number of occasions, just to be sure the weeds were kept cut down." He was very good with his hands and loved gardening. He tended to the gardens around the house, keeping them nurtured. That was why they were so beautiful. After that first summer, he used to visit Le Grande Manor every year and became interested in gardening. In fact, he received his degree in botany and had owned a nursery for many years. He assured Crystal that the carousel was in pretty good shape.

"I'm amazed. Why didn't you ever tell me you had been going down there?"

"I knew how sad it made you to think about what

had happened, and I didn't want to make your pain any worse. I knew that someday, some way, everything would be resolved. I am just so happy that it has happened in my lifetime."

Matt put his arms around Crystal, and said, "Okay, cuz, let's go!"

Watching her grandma and great uncle together made Chloe's heart full. They had a lot of history, and the fact that they looked out for each other had quite an impact on her.

"I'm ready to go. Are you two young kids going to just stand there, or are we going to get this show on the road?" Chloe thought she was very clever with her remarks and was happy when they both laughed. "Are we going to have to do the Hansel and Gretel thing, or do you really know where we're going? After all, it did rain, and a lot of mud and things have had years to grow!" She giggled. It had been a long time since she had felt so happy and excited.

"Okay, Miss Smarty Pants, let me show you how we did it here at Le Grande Manor." Matt was cooking on all six burners.

We followed him as he made his way down a path that looked like it had just been cut. There was gravel or some sort of pebbles on the surface. The weeds and small trees had been trimmed back making our journey much easier than we thought it would be.

"Matt, when did you do all of this?" Crystal was

amazed at how well everything looked.

"You may not believe me, but I had absolutely nothing to do with this. Honest. I am as surprised as you are."

Just then, a big black raven swooped down in front of them and stopped in the middle of the path.

"Cecil?" All three said together.

Well, we know what happened. The raven turned back into Cecil, looking the same as he did fifty years before. Still a boy of about fifteen, wearing – tennis shoes!

"When did you come back?" was Crystal's question. "Did you do all of this work on the path? How did you know we were coming down here today?"

"Whoa! One question at a time. I never left. After I was returned to the life of a bird, I decided to explore again. I had a lot of help on the path, but I promised I wouldn't reveal my sources, so you will just have to leave it at that, okay? I knew you were coming here today, because we have quite a great communication system. We are in the 21st century, after all." And he laughed, his eyes twinkling. "It is very nice to meet you, Miss Chloe. I understand that you are going to be the one to finally reunite Crystal Ann with her father. May I say, that you look very much like your grandmother did when she was your age; a very pretty girl. But, enough of that, let's get on with the show."

"Hey! Where have you all been?" The familiar voice caused Matt to run down the path right into Jonas.

"OMG," yelled Chloe. "Tell me that this isn't happening. Isn't that Jonas? He must be two hundred years old. Hey, he looks really great for an old guy."

"Thanks, Miss Chloe. Miss Crystal, it is so good to see you. I've missed you so much. You are still a real beauty! So, are we going to do this or what? We don't want to miss the sunset."

Overwhelming would be a good word to use in this situation, but with the history of this family and these relationships, we'll just say that it was pretty normal. They all made their way down the path toward the carousel house. Jonas had gone on ahead and when it came into view, they heard the calliope music. Crystal was so emotional, she didn't know whether she could go through with this, or not. Chloe kept close to her, holding her arm. Matt was on the other side of her, carrying the package that he would soon hand to Chloe.

"Listen to the music. It's so beautiful. And look at those horses. I am amazed at how well they have been cared for. Come on; let's take a spin before we finish this task." Chloe jumped onto the moving carousel and held out her hand. "Come on, we'll take one ride. You, too, Uncle Matt."

Crystal was not sure she wanted to do this, but Jonas took her hand and led her to the carousel. He found White Magic and helped her up onto the saddle. Crystal almost had an emotional meltdown, but Jonas gave her a big smile, "Everything is going to be all right."

Jonas waited until they were each atop a horse and made the carousel turn faster. It wasn't like riding a real horse, but it was exhilarating just the same. At the end of the ride, they walked off and stood together, ready for the procedure that would at last reunite Crystal Ann and her father.

Crystal turned around in time to see Cecil climb up onto the carousel holding White Magic's bridle. Surprised, she asked, "What are you doing?"

He simply explained, "I don't belong to this time and these horses will need looking after. I am so glad to have met you and will be grateful to you always for saving me, but don't be sad; I'll keep an eye on all of you from my special place in the universe."

Crystal's first impulse was to hold on to Cecil. In the short time he had been in human form, they had become very close. She knew she couldn't keep him around. He didn't belong in this time, and she couldn't go back to his. "If you meet my parents, will you tell them I love them very much?"

He agreed and stepped back off the carousel holding something in his hand. "Many years ago, I took this gold ring from its owner. I know that was wrong and I am going to return it. Thank you for keeping it in a safe place for all these years. I learned so much from you, Crystal, about doing for others, and I shall never forget you." And with that, he returned to the carousel.

Crystal dabbed at her tear-filled eyes with her hankie. "Thank you, Cecil. Jonas, will you be going with them, too?"

He nodded. "It is going to be so lonely here without you. Thank you for all of your help and for staying around until we could finish this. I shall miss the beautiful calliope music and your great smile."

Crystal hugged him, and Matt and Chloe ran up to join them in a group hug. Chloe looked to her grandmother and she nodded, as if to say it was time.

Matt was carefully holding the paper, and Crystal handed Chloe the sealed incantation.

Chloe looked up at Jonas and Cecil who were standing on the carousel platform. They smiled at her and nodded their heads, indicating that she should begin. Crystal, Matt, and Chloe stood close to one another as Chloe opened the seal. The words were written on parchment with a beautiful hand. She quickly scanned it, motioned that they were to hold hands and face south. Chloe cleared her voice and tried to swallow the lump in her throat.

She began:

"Say these words, and when you do, open your heart and don't be blue. Octowallica-bim-bom, says your mouth, it only works if you are facing south."

The shadowy forms of Crystal Ann and her father appeared and stood next to White Magic.

The scent of gardenias filled the evening and Daphne appeared as an angry child. "Ha! You won't ever be able to put these souls to rest. I won't let you."

Turning to Crystal, she said, "You failed at what you were supposed to do so many years ago. And Matt, look at you. You're just a pudgy old man."

Daphne continued with her wrath, "Chloe, you're no better than your grandmother, or your great-grandmother. No one is as powerful as I am. I can stop everything from succeeding now, just as I did fifty years ago. I hold your family's happiness in my hand, and I want them to experience as much misery as I did in my life. There is nothing you can do to stop me."

Chloe stepped forward. "Look, you selfish little snit! You don't scare me. I read your notebook, and you are a pathetic little brat! My grandma is a great lady, and I love her. She was trying to help a little girl get back to her father, and you prevented her from doing it. But I am not going to be stopped in doing what I am supposed to do, so just step back!"

Chloe continued with the incantation:

"Doo-daffa-dingle-differ is strange to your ear,

but the end result you must not fear. Hiptaminica-wonga-songa-bomptalaria, these words are said by one who is fairer."

The father and child appear more solid. They glanced around as if getting their bearings.

This only angered Daphne, "I won't allow it!" And she caused a spark to ignite near the carousel. Matt and Jonas ran to stamp it out. Chloe stood her ground, and said, "You can't scare us."

"I'll do more than scare you. You can't do this! If they go, then so will I. We are linked together by my crimes! What will become of me?"

Crystal stepped forward to confront her. "You must say you're sorry for what you did. You must mean it." She continued to work on Daphne. "You were loved. Michael and Crystal Ann loved you."

Daphne screeched, "NO! No one loved me!" She began to cry.

Chloe continued with the incantation:

"Holding hands, you must all engage your honest thoughts and loving care to those with whom you want to share dreams and wishes of years gone by."

Crystal Ann and Michael were solid now. Crystal Ann reached out to Daphne and said her name and that shocked her.

"I'm so sorry. I loved you so much and hadn't meant to hurt anyone. I just wanted to ride White

Magic and when Michael tried to stop me, the lantern dropped, and the hay caught on fire. The beam fell on us." Crying hard now, "I didn't mean to hurt anyone. Crystal Ann, I spooked White Magic and caused your accident. I didn't want that to happen, I just wanted you to notice me. Please forgive me."

Michael said "Of course we forgive you. Now come with us." Daphne stepped up onto the carousel platform, and she was once again the pretty young girl she had been before the fire. Michael held both of their hands as Chloe read the last part of the incantation:

"Rid your thoughts of sadness, and fill your hearts with gladness

Those who have been separated will unite again

Because of unselfish acts and kindnesses shown by a girl with a pure heart, who now finds peace within her own."

Chloe had a difficult time speaking the last few lines, because of the tears in her eyes and the tightness she felt in her chest. She couldn't move and kept a tight hold on Crystal and Matt.

The carousel began to move, and the sound of calliope music filled the night. They watched and smiled at a reunited family finally at peace.

The calliope music grew louder. The carousel shimmered and faded from view with everyone smiling and waving. Then silence, except for the audible sobbing from Crystal, Matt, and Chloe.

Chloe was totally awed by the experience and unable to take her eyes off the site where the carousel had been. Crystal wrapped her arms around Chloe and kissed her on the top of her head.

"I love you, Grandma," Chloe said.

"I love you," was the reply.

Crystal turned to Matt and together they said, "I love you."

Chloe knew she would never be the same.

Epilogue

Sitting at the counter in the old 1950s kitchen, with its faded linoleum and 'funny' stove and refrigerator, Crystal, Matt and Chloe were dunking chocolate chip cookies into large, cold glasses of milk. They had just returned from Atlanta, where Chloe was telling them all about the party. She was more animated than she had ever been before.

"The music was so cool. They had this awesome DJ and played all of our favorite songs. My friends were glad I was there, especially Ryan – he's soooo hot! He said he thought I was very pretty and wants to see me again when I get back from my vacation. It was the best party of my life!"

If she said, thank you once, she said it a dozen times. Grandma and Matt had had their own 'date' and went out to a movie and indulged in hot fudge sundaes.

More than once, Chloe wanted to relate her experiences about Jonas and Cecil and the whole carousel thing, but she said her friends were into the party, and besides, she wanted to keep those memories to herself.

"I can relate to that," said Matt. "When I returned to San Francisco and started telling the story of my vacation to my friends, I was laughed at and made fun of, so I decided that those dum-dums didn't deserve to know. They still don't!"

Chloe dunked her cookie again and smiled at her grandma. "There are so many things I want to know. Tell me all about your mother and father, and their antique store. What happened to it? Do you have any of your father's illustrations? Did you get to study ballet, and if so, were you good?"

Crystal finished her glass of milk, wiped her mouth with a napkin, and stood up, pushing the stool away from the counter. "Let's go back to the attic and see what we shall see."

"All right!" Matt chimed in. He was ready for anything. "Or is this a girl thing?"

"What do you think, Chloe, should we let him join us?"

"Absolutely; as long as he brings the cookies."

As they climbed the eight steps to the landing, they looked up at the stained-glass window. The beautiful flowers smiled back at them as a sign that all was well. The pictures of the ancestors had once again returned to their rightful places in history (wherever that was) and the beautiful landscapes had replaced them, hanging next to Crystal's favorite painting of the herd of wild mustangs; the young colt

233

still leading the pack. It was bittersweet, but they knew that was the way it had to be.

At the entrance to the stairway, they counted the sixteen steps, laughing at each other for doing so. Matt had replaced the burned-out bulb with a brighter one, as he was sure they would still be in the attic after dark. He also put new candles in the tin box, just in case.

The attic remained unlocked now since the mystery was solved and the mistakes had been forgiven. It was a very cozy room, and Chloe was sure there was a lot more to explore.

She had a million questions and didn't know where to begin.

Crystal told her and Matt to pull up a box to sit on, as she sat down on the big cushion that had been there for so long.

"Grandma, please tell me about your parents and their antique shop. I want to know everything about you." Chloe was impatient and wanted to hear it all.

Crystal began, "As a child, my mother was a tomboy like I was, and also loved horses. Her name was Margaret Lynne Le Grande Baxter. I think she could have been Miss America, because she was tall, slim, had gorgeous hair, and carried herself like a queen; and she was extremely intelligent and disciplined. Having a talent for expressing her thoughts, she wrote short stories, and my father did all of the illustrations. She also created 'miniatures', like old-fashioned cameos, to be worn as a locket or displayed in a case. Each one was different – signed and numbered. They were lovingly displayed in their shop and were quite popular. A few of them are on the dresser in 'your room' upstairs. Mother spoke several languages and was equally at home in a palace or rustic shack. She had a wonderful sense of humor, and people loved to be around her. She was thirty-five years old when she died, much too young.

"My father, Carter Taylor Baxter, was thirty-seven at the time of the accident that took his life. He was tall, had big brown eyes and brown wavy hair, and was very good looking. When he and my mother met at college, he was a 'football hero', and all the girls wanted to date him. His heart belonged to my mother from the first time he saw her and that was that! He became a renowned illustrator, and his work had appeared in many famous magazines and books. When he was working at his easel, he became part of the canvas. I think that is why his illustrations were so much in demand. There was definitely something real about them, and you would swear they could reach out to you."

Chloe remarked, "It is no surprise that you could express yourself in your journal. It was inherited from your parents."

Crystal patted Chloe's arm. "I am sure my

parents' talents are appreciated by God, and I am not so mad at Him anymore. I guess He needed them more than I did."

It was not as difficult to relate stories about her parents to Chloe as Crystal had thought it would be. She had never shared information with anyone except Matt, but that was a long time ago.

"My father and mother were quite a team. Their mutual love for art and antiques caused them to open *Once Upon a Time*, a quaint little antique store. From time to time throughout my childhood, my parents had to go away on business trips to buy antiques for their shop.

"Their love for family tradition was very great, and mother said she felt a real connection with the people who had owned the pieces before. Both Mother and Father had a sense for what would sell. They traveled all over the world to find their treasures, and always brought me back some wonderful trinket that depicted the country they visited. I kept them in a special book that had deep pages like a shadow box. It was fun to look at them and imagine myself being there."

"Do you still have them?" Chloe was animated with her question.

"Yes, I do. I took them out of the shadow box many years ago. They are in a curio case in the front parlor. I wanted everyone to be able to enjoy them.

Many of the antiques from their store are in this house. My grandmother closed the shop and had them brought here.

"I want to give you Crystal Ann's birthstone ring, Chloe. Since we all share the same birthday month, it should belong to you now. It is still in the jewelry box upstairs."

Chloe moved over to her grandma and hugged her around the neck. "That means so much to me. Thank you, Grandma."

Crystal kissed Chloe's cheek and continued her story. "I was able to study writing on a scholarship and was in several productions in Atlanta, but my love for ballet wasn't like it was for horses. I never owned a real horse, but the memories I had with White Magic were precious to me. I don't know for sure, but I think the horse that Cecil, as the raven, rode onto this estate was really White Magic. Many times, I wondered whether White Magic may also have been killed in the fall, and his spirit ended up on the Ashford Estate, in order to connect with Cecil. Perhaps that was why Cecil came here. Remember, that the white horse disappeared once the raven found the carousel. I have often believed that there was more than a coincidental connection between the two of them; White Magic and Cecil. I know it sounds way out there, but after all of the strange things we went through, nothing would surprise me.

"I have all of my mother's stories and my father's illustrations in leather-bound albums in the front parlor. I hope you will take the time to look at them. We'll do it together if you like."

"I'd love that."

Between bites of chocolate chip cookies and hours of questions and answers and laughter, Crystal and Chloe's relationship had grown to the highest level of respect and love.

Matt was still Matt, a devilish but loving man, who still called Crystal, 'Cuz', and was the life of the party, as usual.

Once again, as they looked at the items from the past, the importance of family came into focus. Loving hands had carved horses, both large and small, and the meaning of those actions intensified the love that a parent had for his child. No less important were the photos and needlepoint and small pieces of jewelry that all had a connection and impact on this family. No matter how much time elapses, memories will still fill our minds and our hearts. What we do with the time we are here on this earth will be remembered. What may seem like a tiny act of kindness may fill another's heart with immense joy. We should never sidestep responsibility, but welcome it with open arms, knowing that someone will benefit from our kindness.

What would be in store for me in the years to

come? thought Chloe. *There are still nineteen incantations in the attic. Will my ancestors appear again and challenge me to make another journey? Deep down, I wished that would happen, and hoped that Matt would be willing to come back to help me.*

Chloe recalled what her great-grandfather, Carter Taylor Baxter, had told his young daughter so many years before, "No unselfish act, done out of love for family, friend or country will ever go unrewarded."